DO VAMPIRES POOP?
AND OTHER MYSTERIES OF THE UNIVERSE

WRITTEN BY:
MICHAEL TRUPIANO

To Danni,

   I hope you like weird books.

   Michael Trupiano

Do Vampires Poop? And Other Mysteries of the Universe

Copyright ©2017
Michael Trupiano & Radio Galaxy

All rights reserved. No part of this publication may be reproduced, stored in a retrieval system, or transmitted in any form or by any means, electronic, mechanical, photocopying, recording or otherwise, without the prior written permission of the author.
This is a work of fiction. Names, characters, businesses, places, events and incidents are either the products of the author's imagination or used in a fictitious manner. Any resemblance to actual persons, living or dead, or actual events is purely coincidental and unintentional.

Story created and written by: Michael Trupiano

Story Edits by: Michael Trupiano

Cover by Radio Galaxy Creation and Design Department

CHAPTER INDEX

THE QUESTIONS

1.
WHAT WOULD HAPPEN IF A HORSE DIED STANDING UP?

2.
WHAT WOULD HAPPEN IF YOU SURVIVED A COCAINE OVERDOSE?

3.
WHAT IS THE THIRTY-SEVENTH BEST USE FOR AN INVISIBLE CAR?

4.
HOW WOULD SUPER POWERS AFFECT LAW ENFORCEMENT?

5.
WHAT IS THE WORST TIME TO GET PIZZA?

6.
HOW MANY SUPERVILLAINS DOES IT TAKE TO ROB A BANK?

7.
HOW DO THE RUSSIAN MAFIA KIDNAP PEOPLE?

8.
WHEN IS THE WORST TIME TO START HEARING VOICES?

9.
DO VAMPIRES POOP?

10.
MYSTERIES FROM A TO Z

This book is dedicated to making Dixie smile

THE QUESTIONS

The Universe is a vast and mysterious place. Many questions wondered go annoyingly unanswered and lost to the annals of time. This book holds one specific purpose and that is to answer a very specific question about the digestive functions of a mysterious variety of person. This book holds the answer to a long asked question about the ever cryptic sub-species of human known as the Vampire.

Given that a vampire has a liquid diet, that bares the question, pondered by many and researched by few... Do they need to poop? Or is their butt mostly for decoration?

Some would say the answer to that question depends on the type of vampire. Are they a magic vampire who draws their restorative and supernatural power from the blood? Perhaps they contracted a blood born virus? Then again, what if they were simply a mistake of science?

This book seeks to answer this ancient question, along with others, by simply taking a short trip through the stories of extraordinary people. Stories of a journey in which we will bring light to a number of mysteries of the universe.

What manner of mysteries would that be? One such example would be: Where does the name mortician come from?

Well, it is actually the male version of Morticia, which is the Slavic word for night lady. Back in their native Slovenia the night ladies were women who would sneak into your house in the middle of the night to take away any dead bodies you had for burying.

The modern male-centric world has since changed the word to make it more fit for men. Additionally the job now ensures that Morticians, or night fellas, are confined to funeral parlors. No more stealing bodies in the middle of the night.

Could you imagine if grandma died peacefully in her sleep and then by morning her corpse was gone? The only thing left behind being an open window and a thank you note on her pillow? No, my good sir or madame. That is not a world I would want to live in any more.

While that is no longer the way of the world, in most places, it is neither here nor there. However, in the here and now, as the title postulates, by the end of this book we shall finally lay to rest that question of old: Do Vampires Poop?

1.
WHAT WOULD HAPPEN IF A HORSE DIED STANDING UP?

The question posed by the ages of myth themselves seems simple. While it would be quite easy to give just an answer, that would not give the answer credibility or backing. No, this answer requires more. There is a story behind the events that lead to the answer we seek. Characters that set events in motion to solve this query.

Do not be disheartened if there are no vampires to speak of right off the bat. They will show themselves in time but for now we go to a small farm set in a hilly valley of middle America. A man named Derek Snyder rode his motorcycle towards this hilly farmland because the hills were most fun to ride his dirt bike over. He never got permission to do so but he knew Barb, the old woman who owned the place, and she never seemed to mind.

It was a pleasant Saturday morning as he drove down the winding roads, listening to National Public Radio on a headset built into his helmet. There was a famous forensic scientist who had been studying vampires but he was publicly shamed at a conference in Virginia about his theories. Apparently he was of the crowd that believed vampires pooped and this was an unpopular opinion. Most scientists in the field were certain that all waste the vampire's digestive tract produced was excreted through urination, and so the scientist was shamed. Not one vampire, to this point in history, ever discussed their bowel movements with any who were not vampiric, so he had no evidence or even reputable hearsay to report. Silly as it may seem, vampires turned to ash once dead and living vampires were less that cooperative on an operating table.

Derek chuckled to himself as he listened in to the radio, deciding to himself that they probably did not defecate. As he rode down the road, on this same Saturday Barb's son Rich, had come to visit. Barb was concerned one of her horses was sick. She said he'd laid down on the field on Thursday and she hadn't seen him move much since.

When Rich arrived he saw the horse had not only died on it's feet but then fell over on it's back afterwards. It was laying with all four feet up in the air like something out of a cartoon. He wasn't sure if she was joking when she said the horse was a bit under the weather, but he set out to take care of it either way.

He rode the old green tractor out of the barn and started wrapping a chain around the inflated carcass. Two days in the sun didn't do the dead horse any favors. The twelve hundred pound beast was bloated with gas trapped in it's decomposing body making the corpse bloated and fat. He managed to get it tied off and hooked up to the rear of the tractor then set off.

Rich drug the horse's body over the hills of their farm and found a somewhat secluded spot. He unhooked the bloated horse long enough to use the scoop on the front of the tractor to dig a rather deep hole. Once he was sure that the hole was deep enough, he used the scoop of the tractor to push the horse in and then cover it with dirt afterwards.

Satisfied with his work, Rich returned the tractor to the barn and then returned to sit with his mother on the back porch of the farm house. She had a glass of lemonade ready for him as they sat back.

"Well at least he didn't die in the barn," Barb started off.

"True," Rich sighed, "That would have been a mess."

"How would you have even gotten him out if he did die?" She wondered, "You'd have to of taken out one of the walls."

"No," Rich sighed again, "I would have had to spend a day with a chainsaw, seeing things I really don't want to see."

The sound of a dirt bike echoed through the hills as Derek sped down the road towards the hills of the farm.

"Who is that?" asked Rich as he saw the man go off road and down into the hills along their field.

Barb chuckled, "Oh that's just a young man who comes down to ride his motorcycle on the hills. He's not doing any harm to no one."

"Well, no. I 'spose not..."said Rich as he heard the sound of the dirt bike as Derek jumped over the smaller hills, riding up and down every which way, "But I just buried the horse out there."

It wasn't long after that they heard the dirt bike stop suddenly as a sound echoed across the hills which could only be described as mix between a large pop and a fart. A moment later they heard Rich scream and the shrill shriek echoed throughout the valley. Trees and plants turned black and withered fast. Barb and Rich heard the sound of his scream and it resonated in them.

Barb looked to her son, "Your ears are bleeding..."

Those words were the last thing either of them heard as the valley died.

2.
WHAT WOULD HAPPEN IF YOU SURVIVED A COCAINE OVERDOSE?

Steve Jablonski wasn't ready for a day like the one he was having. Given the day he was having, few would have been. He was in the back of a plane as it took off from a jungle air strip out of Columbia. It certainly wasn't the first plane to take off from that airstrip with a cargo hull full of weed and cocaine headed for the states.

Unfortunately, as it took off, Steve and his pilot were fleeing members of a rival cartel who were armed with sub-machine guns. The plane was coming under heavy fire as it took to the air. Fortunately it's hard to aim a sub-machine gun while firing and leaning out of a Jeep at the same time.

The hull was riddled and Steve was forced to dance as the floor erupted up from under him with a flurry of bullets. There was no where to go in the confines of the cargo hold so he jumped atop one of the massive pallets of marijuana. He lay atop the pallet and let it soak up the bullets for him while checking for holes.

There were no holes except the ones in his clothes but the bullets continued to rain on the underside of the plane and more than a few hit some of the bricks of cocaine in there with him. A heavy dust of energy-giving highly addictive white powder soon filled the air in the back and coated Steve.

He tried to calm down but his heart was going a hundred miles a minute even though the bullets had stopped. A cocaine fueled fire burned within him and erupted in his legs as he suddenly shot up from the weed blocks and to his feet as he started pacing through the clouds of white wafted back into the air over and over by the wind coming in through the bullet holes. He marched up to the front of the plane shaking like a paint mixer.

"Cocaine everywhere!" Steve Shouted.

The pilot looked back as the cocaine clouds wafted to the forward cabin, "Jesus, Steve. Dip into the product a bit, did ya?"

Steve looked at himself, noticing that he was now coated in a fine white powder dusting, "Shit. Do we have any wet wipes or something?"

"You're not flying Aeromexico, in case you didn't notice," the pilot replied, "You hit?"

"Don't think so!" Steve shook his head, shuddering with the high of a thousand lifetimes, "But there's cocaine everywhere back here!"

"Patch the holes with somethin' ya moron," said the pilot, "It's just gonna keep blowing around."

"What the shit am I going to patch it with? Weed?"

"I don't know," said the pilot, "Just find something."

"Did they nick the fuel?" asked Steve.

The pilot checked the meters on his controls, "Fuel levels are holding steady. If they hit the tank or the lines we'd be seeing it drop off kind of fast."

Steve nodded and started to jitter as he talked faster and faster, "I'm gonna shove something in those holes so we don't inhale all the product before we hit stateside. I know we got shot at a whole bunch but I feel really good about the rest of this flight for some reason."

Cocaine acts as a stimulant and ordinarily, with an

ordinary sized dosage, the person would experience the peak of the effects in thirty minutes. However, in a saturated environment the effects could last longer, especially when on borderline over-dosage for hours of travel in a stressful situation.

The drug effects each person differently, but in the case of Steve Jablonski, after he finally made it back to the states his bosses decided to give him five days off for recuperation. It was five days without sleep. Still full of energy, they called him back in.

They sent a car for him that morning, to his small apartment in San Diego. As he got in the black sedan with tinted windows, there was a bleach blond British man in a black suit already in the back of the car.

"Well if it isn't Mr. Jablonski the mathemagician himself," smiled the Brit.

Steve scootched into the car and the driver closed the door for him. He watched the driver walk round front then looked to the British man's clean cut suit before back to his own disheveled and mis-buttoned suit. He adjusted his shirt to look more proper, "I'm sorry, I thought that I was meeting with Orlov directly."

"Oh, you are," smiled the British man, "But while you were gone he hired me as an intermediary. The name's Pritchard."

The car started and was underway as Steve replied, "Just Pritchard? No first name?"

"None that you need to know of. Think of it as a mononym," Pritchard pulled a cigarette case from his suit jacket, letting Steve get a good look at the gun strapped to his shoulder. He took out a smoke and offered one to Steve, "Care for a fag?"

It took Steve a moment to remember that fag was the British slang for a cigarette, "No thanks. I don't smoke."

"Fair enough," said Pritchard as he snapped the case

shut and replaced it in his pocket, "Do you know what this meeting is about?"

"Columbia and the cartel I assume," said Steve, "But all I did was go there to check inventory and work the books. I didn't have anything to do with the attack."

"On the nosey and we know you didn't, but the boss still needs to see you in person," Pritchard smiled, sparking up his cigarette. He then pulled a blindfold out from a different jacket pocket and tossed it to Steve, "Here, you know the drill."

Steve sighed and donned the blindfold as he and Pritchard were transported to a location that was to remain a mystery to the mathemagician. After he got out of the car clumsily, Pritchard removed the blindfold to reveal that they were at a worn down, rusted over, warehouse at a port he didn't recognize. Not that he was supposed to.

A few guards were posted at the entrance and as he disembarked, they held the door open for him. Steve and Pritchard walked in to see there was a poker table in the middle of the large building. One man sat behind the table and had several more guards standing behind him.

Steve approached with bloodshot eyes. Exhausted but unable to sleep, he stood before his boss, Yegor Orlov.

"Steve," Yegor began, "Been a while. How are you?"

"A lot of sleepless nights, Boss Orlov," Steve replied.

"Nervous about needing to pay back for that coke you huffed?" Yegor smiled.

Steve stared wide-eyed, "Not exactly. I haven't slept because the coke they shot in that plane is still keeping me going."

Pritchard approached the Boss and offered him a cigarette. Yegor took one along with the light that his new intermediary offered. After a puff of smoke he asked, "You haven't crashed? Is bad for you to no sleep."

"Yeah, that has me worried too," Steve nodded,

"Did you say pay you back for the coke?"

"But of course. The product is expensive. We aren't running a charity here."

Steve was running eye zaps and microsleeps and after so long awake he wasn't sure the things he was hearing were really the things he was hearing, "I shouldn't have been sent to Columbia. You sent me there to check the books and I ended up almost dying. I didn't snort or shoot up that coke. It was shot at me with bullets till it was in my eyes and everywhere involuntarily."

"And we apologized for the mix up at the airport. Affairs have been settled. People have been dealt with," Yegor began, "But to fix situation, there must be one final pay off made. They want you to make it and will accept no other. Only you."

Yegor snapped his fingers and one of his guards brought over a metal suitcase. The boss took some keys from his pocket and opened the case, then turned it to face Steve. It was filled with cash. Bundles of hundred dollar bills filled the case to the brim. He closed the case, set the keys on top along with a set of tickets.

"If I do this then we're square?" asked Steve.

"You do this and we are on the road to being square," said Yegor as he slid the case with the keys and tickets over to Steve.

Steve took a look at the bus tickets. The top ticket went all the way to Maine, "Where exactly am I going?"

Yegor smiled. "Ticket is to Maine but you will be going part of the way with this for exchange. A man with a red suit at the rest stop in Gothenburg Nebraska will give you another case and you will trade tickets with him. Then you get on his bus with his case and you will bring it back here. Easy enough, right?"

"Sounds easy enough," said Steve as he took the case, keys, and tickets in hand.

"Better get going. You have a bus to catch," said Yegor with a smile as he sparked up a cigar.

Steve was escorted out of the warehouse by Pritchard, and he was brought back to the car. Scarcely a word was had as they took him to the bus station. Microsleep was taking it's effect on him as, after so many days without sleep, he started to finally fade.

He made it to the bus stop and after a few short hours wait, he was able to board his bus with case tightly in hand. He walked to the back and managed to take in the view for a bit, but the rocking sway of the the big bus took it's toll and escorted him off to dreamland as the crash had finally hit and hit hard.

Steve had pleasant dreams and wandered through a magical land. He was a flying wizard with powerful magic and a majestic beard the likes of which he wish he'd have been able to grow when he was awake. He had to go fight the evil dragon Zorbulak and rescue his princess fiancee. He took a long look in the mirror observing his sleek brown hair and green eyes. His face was just as it was in his life outside the dream, except for the beard, and much like in real life he had a disappointing bit of extra pudge that he never seemed to be able to get rid of.

He ran to the window and flew off into the night sky, riding into the storm. Steve was ready to fight Zorbulak and his fire hordes but that was when someone nudged him on the shoulder. He stirred but then slipped right back into the dream.

The second nudge wasn't gentle. It was more of a jostle. That's when he woke up in a bus depot. It took a bit for him to come back to reality as he wiped the drool from his mouth. Steve looked up to see a uniformed man. It was the bus driver.

"Hey man. End of the line. You gotta go," said the driver.

Steve looked around, "What? Where am I?"

"Landlake City," said the driver, "You gotta get off my bus. You're not supposed to be in here still."

"Oh shit... how far is that from Gothenburg?"

"I don't know where that is, man."

"Nebraska."

"Holy crap dude," the bus driver chuckled, "Nebraska was like two days back."

"Shit! Shitty shit shit..."

"Shit's right if that's where you needed to get off," said the bus driver, "Speaking of... you got to go man."

"Why didn't anyone wake me up?" asked Steve.

"Man... I ain't nobody's baby sitter. You're a grown ass man."

"What if I was dead?"

"Wouldn't have been the first on my bus," said the driver, "Seriously though, get your ass out the seat and off my bus. My shift ended twenty minutes ago."

Steve checked his immediate surroundings and saw, with a sigh of relief, that in his sleep he had laid on top of the metal briefcase in his cocaine fueled mini-coma. There was an impression on his face that confirmed he had been sleeping on it for some time.

He managed to get his lethargic legs out of the seat and stood weakly to his feet. He clutched the suitcase to his chest as he walked off the bus he realized just how hungry and thirsty he was after not having eaten or drank anything in a few days. Steve's stomach made noises he had never heard before as he walked off the bus and into a large parking lot filled with identical buses.

He walked out of the fenced in parking lot and came out on 36th avenue. Not the best neighborhood to walk through with a metal case full of money. Lucky for him there was a diner across the street and bad neighborhood or not... he needed some food. He set the suitcase atop a broken newspaper dispenser, unlocked it and took out a few hundreds.

When he closed the suitcase and locked it again, he felt his phone vibrate. After a few days he was surprised it had any battery left at all.

Two percent battery. Two hundred and three text messages. Ninety-seven missed calls. He thought for a moment. Steve looked at the suitcase and took a good long think about just what was going to happen to him if he even tried to explain what happened to him... or the money he had with him. These people were very prompt about money and Boss Orlov wasn't known for being forgiving.

He made a decision, pulled a paper from the broken stand then headed to the diner to check the classifieds for apartment listings.

3.
<u>WHAT IS THE THIRTY-SEVENTH BEST USE FOR AN INVISIBLE CAR?</u>

I know what you're thinking... where are all the vampires? For the time being, they are lurking in the shadows, still in wait of nightfall. Before they make an entrance there is just one more bit of exposition that must be established first. That being said, I can tell you that they are coming and by the end of this book, the mystery of their bowel functions will be resolved. As this story unfurls, the city where it happens and the characters involved fall into place. Fires of ambition burn with a new supervillain who sought to make himself known.

In Landlake City there were superhumans. Heroes and villains and those who sought to make a name as either one. This story begins with a villain who had made a name already paired with one who had yet to do so. The villain who sought to make a name for himself went by the moniker of Death Shriek but for this venture, he was merely the getaway driver. Though he went by Death Shriek, he was often called D.S. by his friends in the supervillain community

Death Shriek was a Caucasian man of average height and build. His costume was black and white spandex with a swirling motif that wrapped around his body. He wore black combat boots and thick, elbow length gloves. His black mask covered his face and neck, but left his mouth and eyes exposed. His black-dyed hair was a foot long and spiked straight up out the top of the mask that wrapped all the way around his head. On his chest was a black and white picture of a mouth screaming with little white sound waves emanating off the sides.

He sat in his car, in the parking lot outside the Clementine National Bank and was only brought in on this job because of the special car he inherited. The vehicle was invisible to any who didn't carry a special medallion that looked like a simple gold tie pin with the letters RS embossed across it. The car was built for speed but, because it was invisible, it was also armored as people often ran into it unintentionally.

The villain of more prestige, who wore one of the special RS pins, went by the name of Lucky Devil. He was a handsome man who wore an expensive red suit and tie, with a black silk shirt, and black eel leather shoes. He looked like an ordinary white man with bright red hair, a pointed goatee and a curled mustache. The main thing that signified his namesake were the three inch long horns that protruded from his forehead.

He tapped a black ivory cane on the ground as he tap danced up the bank steps and into the front door, holding the door for an old lady as she made her way out. As he sauntered his way in he pulled three red dice from his suit pocket and flicked one to the ground.

Tick tack tick tack it bounced across the floor, but no one noticed the die. Then the bank manager exited his office.

"Dianne could you get me a copy of... Hwooop!" as he slipped on the die he fell back. The ground was very unforgiving despite his fat acting as an extra cushion on the landing. He was unable to move after he hit the hard floor as his back had gone out and the series of unintelligible mumbles didn't help, but it did grab everyone's attention. The tellers, the security guard, everyone.

That's when Lucky Devil flicked his second die behind the teller counter and hit the button to start the vault opening. He leaned on the counter as one of the tellers returned along with the security guard.

She ran behind the counter, only to slip on the die on the floor back there. That's when he started to mosey his way over behind the counter himself.

"Hey! Stop right there, mister!" said the overweight security guard. He put a hand on the holster where he had his night stick.

Lucky Devil looked over his shoulder with a grin then flicked his final die towards the floor, it bounced with a loud clack, then hit the security guard square between the eyes. The guard hit the ground out cold and Lucky Devil caught the die again. He walked into the vault with an upbeat whistle and a skip in his step.

He grabbed two sacks of money that had been leaning on the vault door and, hefted them over his shoulder, and proceeded towards the egress. Money over one shoulder, cane over the other, and he couldn't have been more casual about the whole affair.

A burly bank customer in overalls and a red flannel shirt walked up to the horned man as he made his way to the exit, "Hey, what the hell do you think you're doing? You can't just take that money."

"Oh I beg to differ," Lucky Devil smiled and with a quick swipe of his black ivory cane, across the temple of the burly man, and his way to the egress was no longer blocked. He sauntered out just as easily as he sauntered in.

He made his way down the steps to the invisible car in wait, knowing full well that no one else could see it but him, then opened the back door with a final look to the bank. He gave a tip of his hat to the on lookers then took his seat and closed the door, effectively disappearing from view of everyone looking.

Death Shriek looked into his back seat, saw his passenger and then the huge bags of cash, "Wow. That was quick. There's nothing on the police scanners about this yet either."

Lucky Devil cast him a gaze as if to say 'so what?' but then actually said, "Shut up and drive."

Not wanting to lose his cut of the money, Death Shriek did as he was told and go them out of there with a minimal number of accidents in the invisible car. His cut was left on the seat as Lucky Devil skedaddled on to bigger and better things.

D.S. was then left to his own devices. He drove to the parking garage where he stowed the invisible car and then made his way to his apartment. He wondered if his roommate would find it funny if they ordered pizza with his recent cash influx.

One might think that he'd have changed out of his supervillain outfit on the way to his apartment, but one would be wrong. He was an unknown so he might have just of easily been mistaken for a hero as a villain. Despite his achievements he had gone utterly unnoticed though had plans to change that.

He made his way up to the seventh room of the seventh floor and then walked into his apartment only to see, what most would consider, a very strange sight. There was a man dressed like a mod straight from the 1970s only his whole body seemed to be that of a rag doll. The rag doll man's left arm was extended a good seven feet longer than it should have been and casually held up a pudgy man against the wall.

"Death Shriek. Good to see you. A man came to the flat so I invited him in for tea," said the rag doll man, "I'm sorry to say I never caught his name."

D.S. looked at the scene and to the pudgy, brown haired, green eyed man that was effortlessly held aloft by the rag doll man, "Nice to hear, Mod Doll... but a question comes to mind... why did you bring him in here at all? Now we have to kill him."

Mod Doll looked to D.S. with his button eyes, "I thought it was you at the door so I opened it in full villainous appearance, then I pinned him against the wall and not a minute later... here you are."

"I see," said D.S. as he looked to the pinned man, "Well, maybe we can find out a couple of things first. Who sent you here, and why?"

"I was just answering your posting in the classifieds," said the man on the wall, "It said you were looking for a roommate."

"I never put in the address," Death Shriek replied, "Only a phone number. AND it said that only villains need apply plus I already have a roommate. I think you two have met, if I'm not mistaken."

"I'm good with computers. I really needed a room that wasn't a motel. I used to work for the Russian mafia so I figured that was somewhat villainous. You never answered your phone and my name is Steve."

Mod Doll walked over to D.S. while keeping Steve pinned to the wall then whispered, "How much did you make on the job?"

D.S. whispered back, "Enough to buy that place but rent *would* be a bit tight for a bit if any jobs go sideways."

"Mafia isn't a bad background. I've got that truth detector touch so I know he isn't lying. He could take the couch, maybe?" whispered the rag doll man.

D.S. looked to Steve as Mod Doll released him, "Well, we could let you stay on the couch, at least for a while but you'll still need to chip in on a third of the rent. I hope you know that it goes without saying that if you tell anyone about us you'll be killed in so many painful and slow ways it would daunt the mind."

"Better than a hotel," said Steve as he clutched a metal suitcase tight to his chest.

"Right ho then," said Mod Doll, "A few more questions first. Where are you from Steve?"

4.
HOW WOULD SUPER POWERS AFFECT LAW ENFORCEMENT?

All those pages of drug lords, supervillains, exploding horses, and bank tellers but not a single vampire. That is, not a single vampire till this part of the story.

They say that night is darkest just before the dawn and the superheroes of the Remarkables were finding that to be true as they battled the vampire hordes of Count Ursu in the last hour just before first light. They fought across much of Landlake city, through much of the night, in an attempt to keep the powerful vampire from taking over their beloved city for his sired nosferatu. As the night progressed they had managed to take out his entire horde, but not the most powerful of the vampires in their city, Count Ursu himself.

They managed to get him out in the open and as the clock struck 6:50 AM, they only had to keep him out in the open for another twenty minutes and the sun would do the rest. First light was upon them and sun rise wasn't much further off.

They valiantly fought the vampire and the time counted down. During the epic battle, a rather large half man/half pig, dressed like an 18th century fop, crouched down in a nearby alley way next to his sidekick, who was half boy half pig, and dressed in a very similar outfit. They arrived just after having dispatched a few of his horde and were now seeking face time in the main fray.

The sidekick looked out from the alleyway and watched as a man made of shimmering metal fought hand to hand with the vampire, "Golly, Pomp Porker, what do we do now? That Count Ursu just won't stay down no matter what we try."

His hero patted him on the shoulder, "Not to fear, Pip Squeak, it seems that Mr. Molybdenum has the situation well in hand. We just need to keep that dastardly bastard busy for a few more minutes and then the sun will deal with him and all his evilness."

"I don't even know why I'm here!" came the shout of a tiny voice over a tiny megaphone from below the pair of heroes. It was a small woman, no more than six inches tall, who wore a spandex outfit that looked as though it were spray painted in neon-colored graffiti. She held a small megaphone in hand just to be able to talk at a normal audible level, "My powers don't help at all. I fly around and can remove paint from things... I mostly take down graffiti."

Pomp Porker looked down at the small woman, "Professor Gigantic said he needed all hands on deck tonight, Turpentiny. That means everyone in the Remarkables."

"I know the order but then again, I don't see Professor Gigantic around," she remarked.

"That's because he's with the rest of the team sweeping the city for any stray vampires," said Pomp Porker very matter-of-factually before he turned to his sidekick, "Come, lad. Let's show this vampire what we can do."

Without a word, Pip Squeak gave a nod and smile then ran out into the street after his superior. First light was upon them for a while and it wasn't much longer till sunrise. Mr. Molybdenum had just traded blows with the man who looked like he was straight out of a Bela Lugosi movie but was temporarily down after he was thrown through the side of a building. That was when Pomp Porker and his side kick took over the fight.

Pip Squeak ran out in front then charged back at the superhero. He jumped into the air and curled into a ball while Pomp Porker stopped, planted his feet, and thrust out his sizable belly. The sidekick hit him square in the gut then bounced off, firing like a cannon ball right at their vampiric target. Count Ursu only had enough time to turn and see a ball of blubber headed right for him before the lad hit him square in the face and bounced off again.

The Count was knocked into the air, toppling end over end till a taxi cab broke his fall. Ursu rose from the cab, flying up with his arms crossed as he might exit his coffin at night fall and then landed right before the pig crusader. Pomp Porker took a swing at the vampire but as he did, Count Ursu turned to mist so that the fist passed right through him. With Pomp's balance thrown off, the vampire re-solidified and delivered a kick to the hero's side.

He was quite surprised when the pig man didn't move but rather his foot sank into the hefty man's side. Pomp Porker smiled, planted his feet once more, then flexed his fat. The vampire's foot was expelled with such a force that he was flung across the street and sent tumbling to the ground once more.

Count Ursu rose to his feet and everyone watched as the sun came out. The dawn sun was ordinarily enough to send a vampire smoking in pain back to the shadows, but Ursu was unphased. He stood in the light and smiled a fanged grin, watching the hero's expressions as they tried to understand just how he could withstand the ultraviolet rays.

Mr. Molybdenum emerged from the building he was thrown through, the first rays of dawn glimmering on his silver sheen body. He was the first the approach the leader of the vampires, "How is this possible? You can't be in the sun?"

The Count let out an evil laugh, then spoke in a thick Transylvanian accent, "A little bit of time and a whole lot of strong sun screen will do wonders."

He then ran like a flash and knocked the silver skinned hero into a nearby alleyway, where he landed right next to Turpentiny. He started to get up when Turpentiny hopped atop his shoulder, "Hey big guy. I need you to do me a favor."

"Turpentiny, just get out of here. You're going to get yourself killed."

"No no no!" She shouted without her megaphone, "I need you to throw me at blood breath over there."

"That's insane little lady," said Mr. Molybdenum, "He'll gobble you up in a single bite."

She slapped her forehead, "You don't understand. I'm a scientist who has studied every kind of paint known to man. That sun screen he's wearing... there's only one that's powerful enough and it shares some paint-like properties. You throw me at him..."

"And the sun can do what it was meant to."

"Exactly big guy."

"You're sure about this?" asked Mr. Molybdenum, "That flight is probably going to be a one way ticket."

"I'm a superhero," said Turpentiny with an affirmative nod, "This is what I was born to do."

"Pip Squeak! No!" shouted the Pomp Porker.

Turpentiny and Harry looked to see that Count Ursu was holding back the overweight pig man with one hand, while holding up his sidekick with the other hand. The vampire looked to the pig heroes with his eyes glowing red, "I don't usually have pork for my meals but there is always a first time for everything.

His mouth opened wide as he brought Pip Squeak in close. Turpentiny screamed at the silver colored hero,

"Throw me now!"

Without a moment's hesitation he took her in hand and threw her like a dart at the vampire. She hit him square in the face and held onto his nose and ear for all she was worth, "Bla! What the hell? Why do you keep throwing tiny people at my face?"

"I'm not just tiny..." she said as her hands glowed bright green while holding onto his head, "I'm Turpentiny!"

The vampire glowed green for a moment, over his entire body, then returned to normal. With a shake of his head, the tiny woman was hurled to the city street. Her job was done.

The vampire was about to resume his feeding when he started to smoke all over. The sun was now uninhibited and hit him full force. Count Ursu dropped the pig people and fell to his knees, screaming in pain. His skin burned into fly ash, as Pomp Porker delivered a final punch, he exploded into mist that traveled along the city street and went down a sewer grate.

"Whew, that was a close one you guys," said Pip Squeak, "I was almost pork chops for a moment there..."

"Well, my lad, luckily Turpentiny was there to save the day, just in the nick of time too," said Pomp Porker.

Mr. Molybdenum walked up to his fellow heroes, "More like Turp-In-Timey."

His comment then set everyone off in a bout of heroic laughter. That is... everyone except for Turpentiny who was more concerned with the mist that escaped into the sewers.

She tried talking to the three heroes but they couldn't hear her diminutive voice, that's when she pulled the mini-megaphone from her utility belt, "Hey, fellow Remarkables. I don't mean to burst your fun bubble, but the vampire isn't dead. He turned to mist and escaped into the sewers..."

Pip Squeak punched the palm of his hand, "Darn! I

knew we hadn't seen the last of him."

"No no no," said Pomp Porker, "He clearly burst into flames and then exploded when I punched him."

Mr. Molybdenum rubbed his chin, "I don know about that. I mean... I also saw that mist head down into the sewers. It is better to be safe than sorry."

"Yeah, but who is going to go down in the sewers after him?" asked Turpentiny.

As if on cue, a man in a purple spandex suit, that had a white 'U' on his chest along with a helmet that had a fog light on the top, rounded the corner from one of the alley ways and ran up to the gathering of superheroes. By the time he reached everyone he was out of breath and red in the face. He hunched over with his hands on his knees as he regained his composure.

The man in the purple suit looked around to the disappointed heroes, "Sorry, guys. I forgot to plug my phone in last night and didn't realize it was dead till just a few minutes ago. I got here as fast as I could."

Mr. Molybdenum sighed and rubbed the bridge of his nose between his thumb and forefinger, "Way to drop the ball. We could have really used your help tonight, Ultraviolet Raymond."

5.
WHAT IS THE WORST TIME TO GET PIZZA?

Steve was settling in nicely to his new surroundings. He took to the couch with ease and even managed to build a secret compartment into the floor under the couch, to hide his suitcase full of money. He thought it probably wasn't wise to put it in a bank and even less wise to let his two supervillain roommates become aware of it's contents.

Either way, his first month went by in a flash. No sign of anyone from the mafia having caught up to him or even becoming the slightest bit aware of his new living space. As an added bonus he even started to get in closer with Death Shriek. He might even say they were friends by this point.

Perhaps friends would be too comfy a description but at the very least they both liked the same movies, TV shows, and pizza toppings. In point of fact, it was on this Friday night that Steve was chosen to go out on a pizza run. The place was just down the street from their apartment and the only way you were guaranteed to get it booger free is if you went to the shop yourself.

He was just about to leave the apartment but couldn't find his keys.

"Looking for something?" asked Death Shriek.

"I can't seem to find my keys," Steve replied.

"Well that might be because I have them," D.S. replied in turn.

Steve's sphincters clenched all at once, "Why do you

have my keys?"

Death Shriek nodded, "Well, I was wondering what all these other keys were for that are on this ring. I mean I know you have the apartment key but what about the other dozen keys on here? So I was searching for what each of them would go to online. One of them seemed rather interesting, it seems to go to a Sturlight armored briefcase. If memory serves you had a similar case, when you first arrived, but since then it's... disappeared."

Steve was sweating bullets, "So what about the case? What are you getting at?"

Death Shriek walked up close, uncomfortably so, "If you are hiding a supervillain persona, I want you to know that this is a safe place. You replied to that ad for being a supervillain roommate and we're all supervillains in this apartment. You don't have to hide out from us, Steve."

Steve breathed a sigh of relief, "Well... Um... my supervillain side is still... under development. I'm not quite ready to... um... reveal it to the world."

Death Shriek took a step back, "At some point you have to stop preparing for the big reveal and just come out with your evilness."

Steve looked over D.S.'s black and white costume and thought to himself, 'shit... now I have to get a costume too...' he worried about not having a super power but maybe he could just buy a super gun online or something. Either way he realized he was being quiet for too long, "I guess you're right. I just want to make it like... *really good*, you know?"

Death Shriek nodded and motioned to his own costume, "Oh, I *know*. I mean just look at me. So, do you have a super power I should know about?"

Steve swallowed hard and backed up a bit towards the door, "You'll have to wait till the big reveal along with everyone else, I'm afraid. It's still coming together."

"Fair enough," Death Shriek smiled, "Remember I'm holding that big supervillain audition tomorrow night, so if you could reveal your new persona before then, you could always drop by that to try out for the team."

"Right, well I do hope to have something ready by the time that audition comes around," Steve said trying to think of a villainous alter ego for himself.

Steve had almost gotten out the door before Death Shriek stopped him again, "Steve! You forgot your keys."

He turned back absentmindedly and caught the keys easily as he made his way out without another word. On the elevator ride down Steve's mind raced as he did his best to think of a supervillain persona. It probably wouldn't be the worst idea to cover his face up but he had no powers, just a briefcase with about a million dollars in hundred dollar bills. Maybe he could have a money themed costume? He could be the Malevolent Millionaire.

On his way out of the building and down the street he scratched that idea. He chose instead to think of a different persona but as he passed a dark alleyway his mind was led elsewhere. Something called to him with a powerful and wavering thrall...

He was drawn into the alleyway that was directly across from the pizza place he intended to go to. He couldn't see it in the shadow but then suddenly felt a pain in his ankle. The thrall was gone.

He looked down and saw an old hobo chewing on his ankle. Steve tried to kick him off but the old man had a grip. He started kicking the man but he felt weaker somehow.

Steve Jablonski was unable to pull away. He fell over and felt weaker as he looked at the old man, who wasn't looking so old any more. In fact he looked both quite young and familiar. It was the famous vampire supervillain, Count Ursu. Fully recovered after his meal he stood over the weak and dying Jablonski

"Thank you my friend for the wonderful meal. You were quite the treat," said the Count as he knelt before the dying man. He nicked his pointer finger on one of his own fangs then held open Steve's mouth with the other. The blood dripped a few drops into his mouth before the vampire's wound healed itself.

"Am... am I going... to die?" asked Steve as he lay weakly upon the ground.

"No, my friend. You are going to do something else. You will live anew with powers you only dreamed of," Count Ursu let out a menacing cackle, "You are going to be the first lieutenant of my new legion of vampire minions."

"I feel like... I'm dying..." said Steve.

Count Ursu clicked his fingers, "That reminds me, first I should tell you the four things that can kill a vampire. You can die if you are in your solid form and are beheaded. A stake through the heart won't kill you but a spike of leaded iron, two inches below the heart, will. Prolonged exposure to sunlight will also kill the vampire and there is one last thing... vermiculite is a toxic poison to any vampire. Blood is now your food and you will need blood to heal."

Steve was helpless as Ursu dragged him behind a dumpster to conceal him in his weakened state. He laughed maniacally again as he stepped into the city street. Then the vampire suddenly glowed bright purple and screamed as he burst into flames and vanished in a puff of smoke.

A moment later Ultraviolet Raymond ran around the corner with Turpentiny on his shoulder, "Alright. Well that takes care of Count Ursu's evil once and for all."

He held up a hand and Turpentiny gave him a high five, "We did it partner. Now lets go report the good news back to the rest of the Remarkables."

With that they were off, neither of them noticed Steve now completely out if it in the alleyway behind the dumpster. It was several hours before he reawakened, as it were. He rose to his feet and felt tired. Hungry too.

That's when he remembered the pizza. He went to the pizza place but found that they had given his pie away so he had to wait for another to be made. Normally, given as hungry as he was, that pizza would have smelled ever so enticing. However, it was not what held fervor for his appetite. That was back in the alleyway he had come from.

He saw a man holding a woman at knife point as he reached to take her purse. He had already cut his victim on the hand and it drew Steve back across the street once more. He practically floated over.

Steve walked up to the mugger who responded in turn, "Hey man, the hell you think you're doing. Better back off or you're gonna get cut."

The man turned his attention to Steve who walked up almost in a trance while the woman stayed back, not wanting to get knifed. Steve kept approaching and the man stabbed him right through the brown hoodie, right in the gut. Steve didn't seem deterred and he gripped the man, biting him in the neck with new-found fangs. The man was drained and collapsed as he died from the blood loss. One meal taken but there was still a knife in his gut.

He pulled out the knife and bled black blood from the wound. The woman approached him, "Oh thank you, sir. Thank you for saving me."

Steve's blood lust was not so easily sated. He was injured and needed to heal. She was not much of a fighter. He easily took grip of her and drained her in a mere minute. He dropped her to the ground and watched as his wound healed. Then it all sank in.

What had he done? He was a monster now.

"So that's your big secret," came a voice from out of the alleyway.

Steve the vampire turned to see his observer, his face

stained red by his recent meals. That's when he saw Death Shriek. His roommate smiled, "Vampire huh? That is a pretty cool set of powers you've got then. I can see why you'd want to keep that hidden with the huge vampire hunt that's been going on lately."

"How did you find me?" asked Steve.

"You're down the street from where we live?" replied Death Shriek, "You never came back with the pizza and you were acting weird so I came looking for you."

"Well, you certainly found me," said Steve as he wiped the blood from his mouth on the sleeves of his hoodie. His eyes shimmered red in the dim light for a moment and his skin was noticeably more pale.

"Found you out more like it," chuckled Death Shriek, "So about the auditions tomorrow night..."

"I don't have a costume," Steve interrupted. He was still a bit freaked out, what with so recently murdering two people and becoming a full-fledged member of the undead. He didn't want to be dead or wrongfully deadened as it were, but he dare not refuse the offer as he knew what Death Shriek's super power was and did not want to anger him.

Death Shriek blinked a few times and thought on it, "There is an all night costume shop just off tenth and main. We could go there together. Might be a fun night out. They helped me get the parts to make my costume."

Vampire Steve nodded, "Right, well first I guess I should put these bodies in this dumpster over here."

"What? Right here?" asked Death Shriek almost mockingly, "Are you stupid? They'll be found right away."

Steve thought quickly, "Count Ursu was in this alleyway a few hours ago. He fought some of the Remarkables here so they'll blame any vampire related deaths found here on him."

Death Shriek quirked an eyebrow, "How do you know that? Were you already fighting superheroes?"

"No..." said Steve as he lifted the bodies into the dumpster he was left behind with surprising ease. Then he thought of another quick reply, "It's... a sort of vampire sense... thing..."

Once the deed was done D.S. gave a nod, "Right... well about the audition tomorrow night. I was thinking that given your powers that you would be an obvious choice for the team. However, I want you in on the auditioning side to act as a plant. Help keep the other auditioners in line as a voice of reason if it's needed. Maybe help fight them off if a battle ensues or something?"

Steve thought about those words and was still having trouble wrapping his head around being a vampire now, and everything that meant. He never did appreciate the sun. He snapped back to reality from the labyrinth of his runaway thoughts and said, "Yeah sure. Why not?"

With that, the pair of villains were off to the costume shop. Not knowing that just across the street from that store, someone was watching. Someone who recognized Steve. Someone that Vampire Steve would have rather not recognized him at all.

6.
HOW MANY SUPERVILLAINS DOES IT TAKE TO ROB A BANK?

    In Landlake city, a number of years ago, there was a burger place known as Whale Burgers. Their slogan was: 'Our burgers are as big as a whale!' and in reality it was only meant to imply that they had very large burgers. However, their popularity dwindled when tabloids ran an article about them actually serving burgers that had whale meat in them. Soon enough, a gatcha journalist snuck some whale meat into a burger then sent the burger off for testing and not long after they started closing branch after branch.

    Years later, one of the abandoned store fronts still stood as a husk of it's former self. Even though it wasn't in a very good neighborhood, any property in the city was excruciatingly expensive. It was because of that, the supervillains Death Shriek and Mod Doll had a great bit of trouble in coming up with the operating capital to purchase their new secret base of operations outright.

    It was there, on the night in question, where they held their auditions for their soon-to-be super group of villainous individuals. Mod Doll arrived early to rally the villains together and guide them where to go, while Death Shriek arrived a half hour late to make his entrance more memorable.

He took note of the array of cars in the Whale Burger parking lot as he made his way into the establishment. He walked in behind the counter and hit the 'No Sale' button on the cash register. After doing so, an elevator activated and lowered him down a few stories to an old abandoned subway station that was long since sealed off. He looked up to see a trap door close behind him. The subway station had been cleaned up and even had power running to it from the city still. He lowered down on the elevator right into the middle of things.

To one side, Mod doll sat at a long table with two cushy chairs while the seven villains in wait sat on uncomfortable wooden chairs directly across from the table. He took a bow on arrival, "Welcome everyone. I trust you didn't have to wait long."

"Everyone," Mod Doll began, "This is Death Shriek, our leader and future employer to some of you."

Death Shriek walked up to the table and sat beside his roommate, who was reading a clip board with names upon it. There was a good thirty feet between the leaders and the future minions.

Steve raised his hand and Mod Doll called upon him. He then motioned towards the elevator that Death Shriek rode down, "Quick question. Why did we have to take the stairs if there was an elevator this whole time?"

Death Shriek shot him an icy glance, "The elevator is for members only."

"Right-ho," Mod Doll interrupted, "So here is how it shall work: we will call each of you up, one at a time to give us a demonstration in person of what they are able to do and then tell us your schtick. Now. First on the list I have here is: Black Jack Rabbit."

The villain confidently walked up wearing a white, poker-themed, suit that looked like something a high roller might wear at a casino. He really was tricked out with cuff links that looked like playing cards and even the buttons on his shirt resembled casino dice. The only thing that made the interviewers wince was that it appeared he wore the fancy suit over an old worn-out, open-faced, Easter Bunny costume. He was an overweight Caucasian man with a bushy gray mustache, reading glasses, and a big stogie that he puffed on as he walked up.

"Hi. I'm Black Jack Rabbit and I am what you see," he said very plainly, turning around to show off his look.

"That is an interesting choice of costume that you have there," said Mod Doll mockingly, "Why would you wear a bunny suit to a supervillain audition? Did you want to be beaten to death or was there some other end game?"

"It's not just any bunny suit," said Black Jack Rabbit, "It's a super suit of my own design that gives me super strength, speed, and hearing. With the super hearing I'm an expert safe cracker and I made it a bunny suit because I thought that would make people underestimate my abilities."

"I see..." Death Shriek began, "And can you show us these abilities?"

Black Jack Rabbit then squatted down and jumped up two full stories before landing again some fifty feet away, he then ran back over to the table lightning quick and stopped with the sound of screeching rubber, "We good?"

"We good," said Death Shriek. As the latest villain took his seat he proceeded to call up the next from the clip board, "That seems to be the only animal-themed one on our list. The next I'd like to see up here is: Dopplegangster and her devious dopplegang."

A woman in a pinstripe suit rose from her chair and sauntered over to the men at the table. She gave a tip of her fedora and a nod as she simply said, "Gentlemen."

"Ah, a touch of class. Just what I like to see," smiled Mod Doll, "So tell us ma'am where exactly are your henchmen? It says here that you are leader of a group of people, if I'm not mistaken."

"No, that's not what it says," She smiled and then in the blink of an eye there were two of her. Another blink and she went to four then four became eight, "It says that I am a group of people."

"Instant henchmen," Death Shriek nodded, "Color me impressed. I just have to know what the downside is because with a power like that you'd think you would be applying for the Corruption Club or the Sin Society."

"Oh didn't you hear?" one of her dopplegang asked. Another of her gang then replied, "The more reputable super groups no longer take in people with duplication powers. Not after what happened at the headquarters of F.E.A.R."

"I didn't hear about that one," said Death Shriek.

"Well," began the original Dopplegangster, "They had a member named Doctor Duplicate. One day he had a brain embolism in his lab and dropped into a coma but his duplicate power went into overdrive. In just a few minutes, their headquarters filled with brain dead mad scientists till everyone was crushed to death."

"That would be a bad downside, yes," said Death Shriek, "We will definitely keep you in mind though."

She and her dopplegang took a bow. Everyone but the original vanished in a flash as she said, "Thanks sweetheart. I'll just be right over here."

While Dopplegangster took her seat, Mod Doll managed to steal the clip board back from his co-worker. He read off the next on the list but had to blink his button eyes as he read over the name, "I don't see a power here. Just a name. Potted Plant Man."

"That's me!" shouted a young man in hippie clothes and dreadlocks as he raised his hand and shot up to his feet, "I'm *the* Potted Plant Man."

Potted Plant Man walked up in his cargo shorts and

flip flops then gave a twirl as though he were impressive. Death Shriek looked to his partner in crime with a few slow blinks. He then looked to the hippie and slowly said, "Right. I don't know what to ask you here. What makes you think that you would be a good supervillain?"

"Aw man, I'm like totally sneaky. I'm like great at hiding and I could be like the secret spy guy on the team who like sneaks in and just gets stuff done," said the red-eyed man.

Death Shriek leaned in to whisper to his friend, "Can I just kill him now? I mean... come on..."

"Maybe in a while," said Mod Doll to his friend before he turned to the man they were interviewing, "So, again, what can you do? Why should we let you on our team?"

"Alright man. Hold onto your butts," and it was then that Potted Plant Man transformed before their very eyes into a small potted plant. Then he stayed a potted plant for several minutes and neither moved nor changed.

"Okay next," said Death Shriek, "Three more to go on the list. I'm going to say that the next one confuses me. Well, I mean not as much as the incredible Potted Plant Man, but the name on the list is Steve and the power just says Vampire."

It was then that Steve stood up and walked up, dressed in old-timey vampire garb from the costume shop just up the street. He didn't speak but just walked up with a small wave. Death Shriek just shook his head. Where was the effort? This vampire man was supposed to be on his team and he just put down his actual name? Steven then took the opportunity to introduce himself, "Hi. I'm Steve... and I'm a vampire."

It was then that Steve did his best to fly, he floated above the ground and soared at least twenty or thirty inches in the air. He moved very slowly before he turned into a cloud of vapor. With his powers mostly untested he half reformed behind Death Shriek and Mod Doll.

Steve then hopped over in front of them and reformed entirely. His eyes glowed red and stood before them, doing his best to look impressive. Mod Doll then had to ask, "That's nice Steve, but what is your supervillain name? You just want to go by Steve?"

It was then that Jablonski went into another panic. He knew he'd forgotten something. He never did come up with a good name, "The name I chose is: Vampire... Steve..."

"So let me see if I understand this correctly or if I've just gone insane already. You are a vampire named Steve," began Death Shriek, "And your supervillain name is just Vampire Steve?"

Jablonski thought for a moment but his mind was a blank. He could not think of a name and so he just nodded, "Yeah. Vampire Steve."

"Well," Mod Doll began, "It's an original name to say the least."

"It could do with some work-shopping, but we'll let you know," said Death Shriek as Steve walked back to his seat, "So it seems there are only three more to go and the next I would like to see is one with a promising name. I think I'll go with: Back Draft."

A man in a fiery red spandex suit and mask walked up next, "That'd be me. I saw the ones before but I feel I might need to explain my power further."

"This says it is F-Teleportation," said Death Shriek.

"Yeah, about that," began Back Draft, "I want to start by saying it is an extremely useful power and is exceptionally useful as a distraction."

"Teleportation as a distraction?" asked Vampire Steve from behind the villain.

"No, it's actually fart teleportation."

Everyone was silent, then Mod Doll spoke, "I'm sorry. I don't think that I heard correctly. Did you say that your power is fart teleportation?"

"Yes. Yes I did."

"I have no words for that," said Death Shriek.

Back Draft then turned to face the room and back to his interviewers, "It's really a very useful power. You see, I have a near endless supply of... well... farts and I can teleport them from me to anywhere I so wish. It can debilitate anyone with relatively little effort."

"That is the worst super power I've ever heard, and I just saw a man turn into a potted plant," said Vampire Steve.

"Sounds like I have a volunteer," smiled Back Draft.

"You think you can stop me from attacking you by farting at me?" asked Vampire Steve as he rose to his feet.

"I think nothing of the sort," Back Draft began, "I know I can stop you with my powers."

"Fine but if I get to you, I'm going to drink your blood, Fartman," Vampire Steve warned.

"Sure thing, but first thing's first," Back Draft then lifted his leg and grunted, "Tell me what I ate for lunch, bitch!"

Vampire Steve quirked his eyebrow and looked to Death Shriek as he said, "What? How would I know th... oh god. What the hell?" He then burped a horrible belch as the fart had been teleported right into his stomach. It filled his sinuses, esophagus and mouth as the gas escaped him the wrong way. He covered his nose out of instinct but the fart was coming from the wrong side of it and pinching his nose only served to trap it within. He gasped and wretched as he shouted, "White Castle!"

The vampire was incapacitated as he vomited up blood and grabbed his gut. He fell to his knees and was very much stopped in his tracks as Back Draft took a bow for his potential employers, "Ta da."

Mod Doll and Death Shriek couldn't stop laughing as their roommate tried to recover from burping up someone else's horrid fast food fart.

"A cigarette usually helps with fart mouth," Back Draft advised.

Vampire Steve stood up and tried his best to regain his composure, "I'm going to go step out for a smoke. I'll be back in just a few."

"Understandable," chuckled Death Shriek as he watched his roommate go vaporous and float up the stairs to the Whale Burger upstairs. Back Draft, took his seat in the meantime.

The second to last man grew impatient and, before he was called, he ran up next to the potted plant. He looked to be a highly decorated military man wearing black and gray cammo. He was sweating profusely as he jogged in place and shouted at the interviewers, "My name is Major Explosion! Ever since I could remember I always knew that I had the ability to explode and I'm going to show you that right now!"

Without a moment to react the man suddenly exploded in a flash. There was nothing left after he blew up, except a smoldering black spot on the ground. The explosion didn't hurt anyone, but the concussive force did knock the potted plant into the air.

Then Potted Plant Man landed with a crash and his pot smashed on the ground. That's when he turned back, screaming as his legs were mangled from the waist down, "Oh dear sweet Jesus god no! OOOAAaaahhggg..."

He didn't manage to say much else as he passed out from the pain. Oddly enough the explosion radius seemed to have been very contained and the only one hurt by it was *the* Potted Plant Man.

"Do you think he's going to unexplode himself again?" asked Mod Doll.

"I think that a crazy person just strapped explosives

to his body and blew himself up in front of us," said Death Shriek, "I'm pretty sure he's not going to re-materialize."

"Re-materialize! That's the word I couldn't think of," said Mod Doll as he looked to the last name on the list of villains, "Back to business. Last and hopefully not least we have Brown Note."

Brown Note didn't leave his seat. He was a man who wore a spandex suit and mask, similar to to that of Back Draft, only his was brown and with a black musical note on his chest. He waved to the interviewers, "Present."

"Your name and your power are both just listed as: Brown Note. I'm afraid I don't understand," said Mod Doll.

"That's right," he replied.

"Can we get a demonstration of what the brown note is?" asked Mod Doll.

"I'd really rather not give any demonstration of it," Brown Note began, "I really thought it would have been self explanatory. I don't think it would be a good idea to show it off really."

"Well, one of the requirements we put up on the E-Vil website ad was that everyone had to have either a power or equivalently useful talents to apply," said Death Shriek, "If you don't show your power, we can't know you have any use to our organization."

"We haven't seen your power," said Brown Note, "I'd never heard of you before this meeting and you're supposed to be the leader of a super powered villain team?"

Death Shriek stood up and walked slowly around to the front of his table, "Oh I can assure you that I have a power; but also we're not here to assess me. We're here to give you an assessment to see if you are good enough to be a part of our group."

Brown Note crossed his arms, "I really don't think you do have a super power and before I give any kind of demonstration of mine, I want to see it."

Death Shriek walked over the broken Potted Plant Man and kicked him in the gut, waking him up. He whimpered in pain as he lay on the ground, "Please... take me to a hospital..."

"You want to see my power? Fine!" Death Shriek smiled wildly as he looked down to the seriously injured supervillain. He opened his mouth and screamed. A light shined forth in a focused beam, right on Potted Plant Man who began to convulse as he bled from his ears, nose, mouth and eyes. The man bent, cracked, contorted and screamed till his lungs deflated. Then he was silent and Death Shriek stopped his scream.

"See? Death Shriek," said the villain as he pointed to the man in the chair who no longer had his arms crossed, "Now if you would be so kind Brown Note."

"Fine. Just remember that you asked for it," said Brown Note, "I should just give a little warning as I once had the gift of perfect pitch but one day I discovered the brown note by accident and anyone who hears it, shits themselves instantly afterwards."

"Wait what?" asked Death Shriek a bit too late.

"OH!" yelled Brown Note and it was followed by an awkward silence as everyone in the room crapped their pants, just as promised.

Everyone was very still for some time, taking in the situation as Vampire Steve casually walked down the stairs again. He'd missed hearing the brown note apparently as he went back to his seat and sniffed the air, "That cigarette didn't really get rid of the smell. If anything it's worse."

He looked around but no one replied.

Steve waved to his roommates, "Did I miss anything?"

Brown Note looked to him and replied, "Everyone here but you shit their pants."

Steve was relieved, but little did he know, he was in

far more danger now than he was on that Colombian drug plane. The Russian mafia was only just discussing what they were going to do with him once he had been found.

A messenger man entered the warehouse where Boss Orlov was yelling at his assistant, Pritchard. The bleach blond man tried to lay out the current situation, "The Irish have taken out another six dealers this week. We need to focus less on Steve Jablonski and more on this war."

"No!" Orlov yelled, "I cannot forgive his betrayal and I will not give up the hunt for him. He dies because he is the cause of this. He no get to live."

"We're expending too many men searching for him, we need to pull back and focus or we're going to lose everything," Pritchard argued forcefully.

Boss Orlov was not happy, "Are you telling *me* what I can and cannot do?"

Pritchard walked up next to his boss, sighed, and opened a cigarette case, "Here. Smoke a fag. You'll feel better."

Orlov drew a gun and shot Pritchard in the gut. He fell down and the Boss stood over him then unloaded his clip in the bleached blond man. He bent down and picked up a cigarette from the dropped case, "You're right. I do feel better."

He lit the cigarette with the end of his gun and the messenger approached timidly, "Boss Orlov, I'm sorry to interrupt but I have good news. A man in Landlake City spotted Jablonski. He's in a shitty apartment on the bad side of town."

Orlov smiled and then looked over to Pritchard, "Why the hell didn't you tell me that BEFORE I killed what's his nuts?"

"I'm sorry, sir," said the messenger, "Please don't kill me. I didn't know you were going to kill him."

"Whatever," began Orlov, "Get someone in here to

clean up this mess. We're mobilizing to Landlake. I want to see him die myself."

"That's gonna be hard to get everyone down there," began the messenger, "Well, of everyone that's left."

Boss Orlov slammed his fist down on the table beside him, "I don't care if it's hard. We go down there now! Send someone now to get take him alive so I can kill him when I get there. I want it to go really slow."

"I'll get right on it, Boss," said the messenger.

"And no excuses!" said Orlov, "Steve Jablonski will die by my hands!"

7.
HOW DO THE RUSSIAN MAFIA KIDNAP PEOPLE?

The Russian mafia, or Bratva, is the largest organized crime group in the world. It is highly decentralized and more than double the size of the Italian-American mafia. They have ties to drug and human trafficking and make more than nine billion dollars a year in North America alone. If someone in the Russian mafia wants you dead, then you are most assuredly going to die.

Steve Jablonski knew this and was intent on trying to keep from too much exposure, but even as he progressed with plans of super villainy, four burly white men double parked their van in the bad part of town in Landlake city. They double checked the address and headed out as they found the building they were looking for.

A homeless man sat on the stoop outside the apartment building. They approached him and one of the four held up an unflattering picture of Jablonski, "You, have you seen this man?"

All the answers they needed were a few dollars away, but with their first purchase they did learn that this was indeed the apartment building where Steve Jablonski had been living. Within the building Steve and his roommates were none-the-wiser as they discussed the interview that took place just a few short days before.

"I was thinking that the old movie vampire look isn't going to work. Maybe something more modern would be a better outfit," said Vampire Steve to his roommates.

They sat at the small kitchen table with a set of blueprints placed out. Death Shriek looked up first, "Really. You don't think the name could use a bit of tweaking first?"

"I want a mask," said Vampire Steve, "I really don't think I should be showing my face."

"Right," said Mod Doll, "Because you were in the Russian mafia."

Vampire Steve nodded to his roommates, "I was in the Russian mafia and those guys mean business. I did not leave on good terms."

"That's all a discussion for another time," began Death Shriek, "We have the layout for the heist at the bank and in two days, fifty million in gold Krugerrand is going to just be sitting in wait for us overnight there."

"I say that we bring along everyone who survived the interview," said Mod Doll, "I mean, if anyone turns out to be useless then it never hurts to have jail cover."

"I liked Black Jack Rabbit and the Dopplegangster but I could do without Back Draft," said Vampire Steve.

"I thought at the very least, Back Draft was entertaining," Death Shriek chuckled.

"Yeah, well he didn't fart out of your mouth," Steve almost retched at the thought of it again.

"One person I'm gonna say we leave out is Brown Note," Death Shriek pointed out, "I'd rather not shit my pants every time we go out on a heist."

"Right, so we call the survivors back, except for Brown Note," smiled Mod Doll, "But what kind of tasks do we assign to each of them?"

Death Shriek held up a finger as he had just the proposal, "I say we have a meeting tomorrow night, plan what everyone's role will be, then set out the night after and get us our money."

"Right ho," said Mod Doll.

"I'll be right back guy's. I gotta rock a piss," said Vampire Steve as he headed for the bathroom.

Once the door closed, Death Shriek leaned in to his roommate in a hushed tone, "I find that interesting. How far was Brown Note's range? I think this proves something."

"Proves what?" Mod Doll whispered back.

Death Shriek looked to the bathroom door, "That Vampires don't poop."

"What?" Mod Doll whispered back, "That's stupid. Everybody poops."

Death Shriek shook his head, "Robots don't poop. Dead people don't poop. Vampires are essentially dead people so therefore..."

"Not dead. Undead," said Mod Doll in hushed tones, "They eat stuff and therefore you are wrong."

"They eat blood," Death Shriek began, "I say that they urinate but don't defecate."

"I'd bet they do."

"Care to put some money on it?"

Mod Doll rolled his eyes, as well as someone can roll buttons for eyes, "Fine. I'll put a hundred down that vampires poop."

"Only a hundred?" asked Death Shriek, "We're about to steal fifty million dollars."

"I don't have any millions right now and he could poop at any time," Mod Doll pointed out.

"Fine. A hundred it is," said Death Shriek, "Now how do we get him to poop?"

"I don't know that I really want to see it. We could just ask him if he poops?" Mod Doll thought aloud.

Death Shriek shook his head, "No. Anyone can say anything. We need to prove it somehow, like let him eat someone we fed a bunch of laxatives to or something."

The toilet flushed and ended their conversation. Steve walked out of the bathroom just in time for a knock at the door. He looked to his roommates, "Expecting someone?"

They both shook their heads just as the door was kicked in. Four angry Russian men with shotguns burst through the door. The first fired a shell into the ceiling, "Nobody moves and nobody dies! We're here for Jablonski."

"You men seem to have broken into the wrong apartment," said Death Shriek as he and Mod Doll walked up to the four mafia men.

"The hell you talking about, costume boy? He's right there!" he said as one of his guys pointed to Vampire Steve.

Vampire Steve went after the man that pointed to him like a duck on a June bug. He bit the man's arm on the wrist and forced him to drop his shotgun as he started to drain him of blood. The man cried out at he started to feel faint.

Death Shriek stepped in and let loose a scream directed at another of the mafia. The man's eyes, ears, and nose began to bleed as he fell to his knees and his body contorted to unnatural shapes.

The remaining two were looking to unload, one shot Vampire Steve in the chest and it knocked him back. They both fired their shells at Mod Doll but the living rag doll man simply soaked up the damage and kept walking forward. He grabbed them by the neck and threw one into the kitchen. He then wrapped around the other and crushed him till the man's bones snapped in his constrictive grip.

One unarmed member of the Russian mafia remained. He had his phone in his hand and had almost no time to react. He saw the blueprints and plans on the kitchen table so he took a quick picture and sent it fast. The Mafia man recoiled in horror as Vampire Steve floated back to his feet, his gun wounds already healed.

"When I said you had the wrong apartment, I didn't

mean that you didn't find what you were looking for," said Death Shriek, "What I meant is that you picked the wrong apartment to mess with."

"Otva`li!" cursed the Russian, "You're going to die Jablonski!"

Vampire Steve then attacked the man and drank deep of his blood while his roommates stayed back. Death Shriek whispered to Mod Doll, "Double meal. If something's gonna happen fecal-wise..."

Mod Doll shushed him as Steve took notice. He turned to face the others with a mouth covered in blood, "Fecal-wise?"

"It's nothing," Mod Doll assured, "But hey... Russian mafia guys in the apartment. I feel like a wanted man already."

"They're not gonna let this slide," said Steve as he wiped his mouth with his sleeve, "More will be coming after me now. Good thing we have a supervillain team now, right?"

"The rent was paid up till the end of the month, but I say we just move into the new lair ahead of schedule," said Death Shriek, "Oh, and we should probably get Steve a mask like he was saying."

8.
WHEN IS THE WORST TIME TO START HEARING VOICES?

After the attack on their apartment, the trio that led the Wicked Six decided to abandon their living space and move into their secret lair, under the abandoned restaurant, permanently. Steve found it easier to secret away his mafia money with his new found vampiric powers and he was careful never to be seen as they moved only the essentials out of their former apartment and into the lair.

They left their furniture and the dead mafia men when they headed out. It was a bit of a rush move and they never checked the phone of the man who managed to send a picture of their plans off to the first person in his contact's list. It was a member of the mafia, who was out in San Diego, and he wasted no time in telling the boss what he was sent.

With no contact back after their men raided the apartment, the worst was assumed and Boss Orlov wasted no time in leading the charge to Landlake City. He and his men loaded up then headed out en force to find Steve Jablonski and kill him in any number of slow and painful ways.

Orlov sat in the back of his limo on the way to Landlake, still days away as he mulled over the beautiful tortures he would inflict on Jablonski. His train of thought was interrupted by one of his higher ups that sat with him in the limo, "So, I've been meaning to ask boss. I mean... I know we are going to Landlake to find Jablonski, but how are we gonna get to him now? He's not gonna stay in that building any more and the city is pretty big."

Boss Orlov rolled his eyes, "I know you are not a thinking man, but we were sent a picture of a specific place. A picture of a blueprint and in the corner it showed part of a plan. Small time man with a little bit of money thinks he can pull a job off."

"We know the location where he might be, but we don't know when he will be there," said his man.

"When we get there, we lay low," Orlov began, "Have some guys stake out the place and when he shows up we move in. If there is money to cover our losses while we are in the bank, then I say it is a win win situation."

While the boss laid out his plans over their long drive to Landlake City, in the secret lair under the old Whale Burger building, the Wicked Six laid out plans of their own. Led by Death Shriek and Mod Doll, the others who made the cut were Black Jack Rabbit, Back Draft, the Dopplegangster, and Vampire Steve.

Vampire Steve had updated his outfit to look more like a reject from an Underworld casting call, complete with a metal masquerade mask to conceal his identity.

Death Shriek had a holographic display projected into the center of the room, which had a full layout of the bank in question, the First National Bank of Landlake. He motioned his hands through the levels of the bank, showing that there was the main reception on the first floor, but that the Krugerrand were being stored in a vault in sub-basement three.

"On the first floor of this seventeen story building is the night security staff. It's closed to the public when we're going in so Vampire Steve will turn to fog, go in under the doors and unlock them from the inside to avoid any alarms too soon," Death Shriek began. He looked up to Vampire Steve, knowing full well that he'd been over the plan before, yet Steve was distracted, "Vampire Steve, are you paying attention at all? This is one of the parts that involves you."

Vampire Steve looked up and nodded, "No. I am. I've just got a bit of a headache is all. Must be some bad blood I had for lunch."

However, it was not anyone he'd had for lunch. There was a quiet rustling in his mind that was building to the noise level of a large crowd. So many voices that he just nodded and acted like he was paying attention, even though he could hear nothing Death Shriek was saying.

Suddenly the voices quieted to a dull roar and then nothing except for one that rang out directly to him, "Stephen. Hear me. Hear the call of my voice and my voice alone Steven Schiffgenachtmittungstein... Holy hell that's a mouthful. That can't be a real name."

"It was but I changed it," Steve said aloud.

"Changed what?" asked Death Shriek.

"My name. I changed it."

"That's great but we're kind of in the middle of something," Death Shriek reminded by pointing to the hologram again. The plan was still being explained as the voice in Steve's head cut in again.

"Whatever your name is, hear me my child and hear the call of your kind," rang the voice, "I am your king. I am the first to bare our cursed blood and I call you to me for your indoctrination."

Steve was silent, while he pretended to pay attention to the plan being laid out and not the voice in his head.

"Respond, my child, and tell me that you understand," said the voice.

"I understand," said Steve.

"Well, that's one of us then," said Black Jack Rabbit,

"How are we going to keep those third sub-floor alarms from going off? That's gonna seal off the whole place."

"Very good," said the king of vampires, "You shall come at once. As you were the last remaining who was sired by the late Count Ursu, you are to take over his position. You shall assume his responsibilities and so I grant thee the title of Count Schiffgenachtmittungstein... I'm sorry, you said you changed your name? There has to be a better name to call you."

"Could we not do this right now?" asked Steve.

Mod Doll looked to him strangely, "Not do what? Plan a bank heist?"

"Sorry," said Steve, "I don't have a reason for what I said. Please continue."

"Right," said Death Shriek.

As the supervillain went back into his monologue, the Vampire King resumed his speech, "Do you know who I am? King of all vampires? You do what I say when I say it. My whim is your greatest desire to fulfill. Your master may have died before you were bonded to the network that enthralls my children but you are still mine to command."

"I'm busy," Steve said under his breath, luckily with no one noticing. An ordinary man might find all of this concerning but with all the recent going ons that had fallen upon Steve, it was becoming normality.

His vision blurred and the form of a tall man in a dark cowl appeared before him, but only to him, "Don't think for a moment that because your link was severed when your sire perished that you can disobey me."

"Go away," Steve said under his breath. As if by command, the image of the vampire king was gone. He looked around but there was no trace of him, "Wait... can I just tell you to stop talking to me and because I don't have this connection... you have to stop talking to me?"

There was silence in his mind for a moment before a

very unsure reply came in the form of a, "Nnnnoooo?"

"Right," Steve whispered to himself, "Stop talking to me in my mind, or popping up visually, or trying any form of psychic location whatever it is that you do."

With those words spoken, the link was severed and Vampire Steve was back in the game.

"So that's the plan," said Death Shriek, "Any questions?"

"I think that pretty much covers all the bases," said Dopplegangster.

"Alright then everyone," began Mod Doll, "This Friday we meet back here at sundown and then we'll all rob a bank together."

Steve was relieved the voices were gone, but worried he didn't hear the final version of the plan.

9.
DO VAMPIRES POOP?

The question this book was made to answer is at long last answered in this very chapter. Do they poop? Do they though? To find out you will have to read on a little further.

For those of you who skipped to this chapter just to get the answer, first of all, congratulations on finding that shortcut. Secondly, I will now provide a short summary of the rest of the book that happened before this so that you aren't left completely in the dark. If you have read the rest of the book before this, then feel free to skip ahead to page 56.

The story starts with a young, purple-skinned, man named Nebulos on the planet Quetrothy in the Hoth'kar Galaxy, previously undiscovered by any Earthlings. He tired of his old life, then decided to head for the stars, and head for the stars he did. He flew to this planet and that having all kinds of crazy wacky adventures.

First he went to the planet Blimflorp and met a tall blue man, Yippers, and they soon became the best of friends. Although on the space ship one day, the engines suffered a major power failure and broke down. Stranded in space, no power and running out of air, the pair drifted on.

They suffocated long before they finished trying to eat each other from starvation. So the ship drifted for a million years until it happened upon a small blue planet, in the skies of the Milky Way Galaxy, named Earth. So the ship entered the atmosphere. With no shielding the ship broke up immediately and one of the still charged spare power cells broke into a tiny fragment that killed a horse while it was asleep... and then the rest of the story happened.

Back to the adventure at hand... The Wicked Six sat in an invisible car parked in front of the First National Bank of Landlake. It was a tall, impressive building that stood fifty stories tall and housed numerous businesses on the upper floors. At night it was secured with four guards in the main lobby, and for the purposes of our robbers, a further two guards in the third sub basement by the vault.

Death Shriek sat at the drivers seat, while Vampire Steve and Mod Doll sat up front with him. Black Jack Rabbit, Back Draft and the Dopplegangster sat in back on that dark Friday night.

"Everyone remember the plan?" asked Death Shriek as he looked over his shoulder to the group in the back.

"You mean the plan that we went over two days ago? Or the plan that we went over yesterday for several hours and then again tonight for an hour before we came here that was really all the same plan?" asked Black Jack Rabbit.

"I think we know the plan, boss," Vampire Steve chimed in, adjusting his mask.

Mod Doll opened his door first, "Let's move."

With that, they were off. The group exited the car and were suddenly visible to the world. They walked the stone steps to the windowless first floor of the building and the pair of tall brass doors that blocked their point of ingress. That was when Black Jack Rabbit took the lead. He pulled a lock smithing kit from his suit and set to work.

Across the street two men sat in a car and watched the bank. They saw the six supervillains appear from nowhere. The men had a short discussion before they determined it must be one's they'd been waiting for. The villains entered the bank as the man in the passenger seat pulled out his phone then made the call, "Tell the boss he was right. Jablonski just entered the bank with some other freaks in costumes."

Those freaks in costumes did make it into the bank

without incident and no alarms were tripped on their way past the point of ingress. Vampire Steve was first through the door and traveled as a mist through the lobby showing just where all the lazer lights were in the room.

Back Draft stepped into the room next and went to work on the guards at the lobby counter, fifty feet away. He stood in the door frame and with a few grunts, the guards were kept all too busy coughing and gagging. While the guards were occupied the Dopplegangster made her way in. As she walked through the room, dodging the lazer sensors, she left duplicates behind as a relay of look outs starting at the entry point, each one holding an Uzi identical to her own.

Then came in Mod Doll. He cartwheeled, rolled, jumped and leaped through the lazer beams to the guards behind the desk. He snapped one guard's neck on his landing while the other he wrapped an arm around and lifted against the wall. He took the key card off his belt and inserted it into a slot on the computer behind him. There was a ding and a with a few key clacks the lazer grid powered down. Next through the door was Black Jack Rabbit, he walked down the fifty foot long lobby of the bank to the counter with a small device clenched in his hand. He went to the computer terminal and checked a few things over.

"Alright, the silent alarm was never triggered, so the jammer was a bit of overkill," he said, placing the device he held down on the counter. The man in the poorly made rabbit suit looked to the surviving guard and asked, "Is the security system a Tekrost two thirty seven or two fifty four?"

The man in Mod Doll's grip struggled for breath and said, "Two... Fifty four..."

Black Jack Rabbit sat at the terminal and went to work, "Alright. I got what I need to work here," he pulled a USB cord from the sleeve of his suit and plugged into the computer. He then looked to Mod Doll with a nod, "We won't need him any more."

Mod Doll smiled and threw the man half way across the lobby, knocking the wind from him. Then Death Shriek walked in and up to the guard. The guard looked upon him, pleading with his eyes, but Death Shriek showed no mercy and screamed at the man. A light from his mouth shined forth and the man convulsed. Blood poured from his eyes, ears and nose then the man suddenly stopped dead.

With the lobby secured, Death Shriek walked up to the main desk and smiled, "All good so far."

"The hell is wrong with you?" asked Back Draft.

"What?" asked Death Shriek.

Black Jack Rabbit threw his hands up, "Don't say things like that. That's the way you jinx things. Don't be insane."

Death Shriek rolled his eyes as the man in the rabbit suit went back to his computer magic, "I don't believe in jinxes or any of that hullabaloo."

"Do you believe in tempting fate?" asked Vampire Steve as he re-materialized, "I think it's best not to."

The rabbit was able to get through the security protocols and a door just off to the left of the security desk opened. He stood from his chair, "Bad luck or not, security and alarms have been disabled from here through the sub basements. We can get into the elevators down now."

Mod Doll looked to the Dopplegangster, "I trust you lot have it from here?"

The Dopplegangster smiled and made three more duplicates of herself. Two of them pulled aside the dead security guards and took seats at the control station. One of them stood by the security door and held it open for everyone while the original said, "We've got this place in hand and if there is any kind of disturbance we'll alert you."

"Primo," said Mod Doll as he and the others made their way through the security doors, down the well lit corridor and to the elevator that took them to sub basement three.

One might have thought that for this particular establishment, the night security seemed light. However, you would also need to keep in mind that there were security guards posted on every floor and while there were only two in the lobby, there were more on the more secure floors. One of those floors being the third sub basement.

In that sub basement was a security deposit vault where a shipment of gold was being kept for a single night before an armored car was to pick it up in the morning. The floor that kept that vault was below the sewer level and had four guards posted at all times. It had power systems, computer systems and even secured sewer systems that were separate from all the other systems from every level of the bank. Cut off from the world to be extra secure. The private alarm system would not contact the police but was instead a direct line to the Remarkables' headquarters and would summon superheroes to the building if they were tripped in any way, shape, or form.

There were two armed guards who were stationed at a desk right next to the elevator and two more who were stationed down the hall and around the corner at the vault itself. The entire curving hall was very well lit and the floors were electrified with a very brief intermission, twice a night, for a half hour period each time so that the guards could take turns using the private rest room.

It was time and the electrified floors deactivated. The first guard, named Todd, knew that he had to go on time while he had the chance so he drank a laxative laced coffee that set his timer. He stood up and just walked out from his post right by the elevator doors when the doors dinged and opened.

Todd the guard was caught off guard when a vampire leaped from the elevator and tackled him to the ground. He was being drank from before he had a chance to call out. From the ground he was able to see as a man who looked like a rag doll attacking his coworker as everything went black.

Vampire Steve rose from the laxative infused guard corpse and his stomach rumbled with a furious tension. He looked to his fellow villains as they left the elevator. Mod Doll dropped another dead guard and then pointed to the corner that led to the final two guards for the vault.

Back Draft worked his teleportation with a grunt and the guards stationed at the vault doors suddenly doubled over. Distraction in place Black Jack Rabbit ran down the hallway at superhuman speed. He hopped over the desk, grabbed both guards and threw them towards the rest of the villains in wait.

A pair of the dopplegang caught the guards and held them firmly in strangle holds. It was then Death Shriek let loose a scream that killed not only the guards but the dopplegang members that held them. The Dopplegangster winced in pain as her duplicates died most painfully.

Death Shriek noticed her pain, "I thought they were just duplicates. Why are you hurting?"

"They are, but they are still a part of me. It hurts when they die," she informed, "Shouldn't you use that power on the guard Vampire Steve killed?"

"Why?" asked Vampire Steve.

"Because he's going to turn into a vampire?" she said as though stating the obvious.

"It doesn't work that way," Steve informed, "Unless they drink my blood too, people I kill won't turn into vampires. They just stay dead."

Vampire Steve's stomach gurgled as someone he ate moved through him at a rapid pace. Mod Doll and Death Shriek shared a glance, waiting to see about the vampiric bowel movement. Mod Doll approached him first,

"Everything alright?"

"That guard I drank is not sitting well..." said Vampire Steve, "I don't know what it was but it wants everything inside me to be outside me."

While Vampire Steve's stomach settled, the man in the rabbit suit finished hacking the controls of the vault, "Hey, I know that everyone is super confident after killing a few guards, but we should get the money and get out."

He gave an accentuated key press and the vault door opened. The dopplegang pulled the door open the rest of the way and moved in, loading up with bags of gold. Each member of the Wicked Six moved in and grabbed bags of Krugerrand then made there way back to the elevator with time to spare on the electrified flooring.

The Dopplegangster stopped in her tracks and dropped her money bags and grabbed her stomach in pain. Something was wrong, "My duplicates in the lobby are dead. None of them saw what was coming but something burst through the door up there right before they all died in rapid succession. We need to be cautious."

In the lobby laid seven dead women. Odd as it may have seemed, the deceased duplicates slowly faded from existence while Boss Orlov and thirty of his best men occupied the first floor of the First National Bank of Landlake.

They spread out while Boss Orlov himself stood behind two of his larger men, that he preferred to think of as bullet shields, right by the point of egress to the outside. He and his men waited patiently for Jablonski, and they were more than equipped to deal with one traitor. Their wait wasn't a long one as the elevator doors dinged and opened.

Mod doll and a number of dopplegang duplicates ran out first while the Russian mafia opened fire. Mod Doll did a good job of soaking up bullets, and the duplicates acted as cover just long enough for everyone else to duck behind the metal counter next to the elevator. Back Draft peeked out from behind the counter, seeing Mod Doll grabbing one man then swinging him into another, ironically like a rag doll. He then did his best to do his worst and started teleporting farts into the stomachs and noses of everyone in line of sight.

The mafia men started to gag and double over, then Vampire Steve made his move, ripping throats left and right. The Dopplegangster created more of her dopplegang then they stood up, firing Uzis and taking out further members of mafia attackers.

The Black Jack Rabbit stayed behind the counter still, as he wasn't as bullet proof and survivable as the others. That is until the mafia men had to reload, then he pounced from his hiding place and ran into action. He used his enhanced speed and strength from his mechanized rabbit suit to punch straight through more than a few of the mafia men himself.

Back Draft fell back exhausted against the counter next to Death Shriek, "I'm sorry man... I've never farted so much in my life. I think my tank is running on empty."

"You did good Back Draft. You did real good. Take it easy for a bit and we'll get rid of these jack offs."

Death Shriek then ran from the counter and past the others, screaming at the mafia men who were distracted in the carnage and had not expected the level of push back they were receiving.

The mafia men were not fairing well against the team of supervillains and their numbers cut down fast. They fought till only five remained. Mod Doll took on two at once, Black Jack Rabbit took another, while Vampire Steve took on the two that stood before Boss Orlov.

Make no mistake, they unloaded on him and emptied their clips again before he was able to take them out. Then only Yegor Orlov himself remained. Yegor shot

Jablonski square in the chest, followed by another shot right to the throat. The vampire keeled over with a massive blood spurt from his neck.

The other villains watched as Orlov turned his gun to them with a grin. Then Steve rose again and knocked the gun from his former boss's hand. He bit him on the throat and drank deep of the old man's blood. He dropped the dying mafia boss to the ground and listened in as Yegor spoke with his last breath, "Trakhat' tebya Jablonski..."

"Menya zovut Vampire Steve."

"Did you just say, my name is Vampire Steve, in Russian?" asked Death Shriek.

"Who the hell were these guys?!" asked Black Jack Rabbit, "What they hell were they doing here? Why were they trying to kill us?"

Mod Doll looked to Death Shriek, neither of whom were prepared to answer such a question. Then Vampire Steve chimed in, "I think they were trying to rob the same bank as us? I mean... they might have received the same information as us possibly..."

Steve's stomach gurgled, reminding him that the mob boss was not sitting well on top of the laxative guard. He was interrupted from digging his verbal grave by the sound of loud, metallic, clomping footsteps from behind the broken doors to the bank. He turned in time only to see Mr. Molybdenum run up the stairs to the bank. Steve received a massive punch to the gut the metal man that sent him flying half way across the lobby and caused the vampire to shit his pants.

The mystery was solved as the liquid brown excrement spewed forth from his black pants legs, leaking down to the ground under him while sliding across the floor. Tried though he did, the gut punch did him in, and the diarrhea continued to fire forth and expel itself from the depths of his bowels, down the legs and out the top of his tight vampire pants. He crawled slowly away from the scene of where he finished dooking it out from the impact of a superhero fist.

The Dopplegangster and her dopplegang opened fire on Mr. Molybdenum and the bullets just bounced off him. He laughed at the effort and walked forth past the bodies of dead gangsters. Black Jack Rabbit ran up and took a swing at the hero but his mechanically enhanced fist impacted with a clang. The hero then grabbed him by the wrist and threw him forth into Death Shriek, knocking them both down for the count. The man in the rabbit costume lay unconscious atop the other supervillain, who was unable to push the man off of him as that robotic rabbit suit was heavier than it appeared.

The dopplegang opened fire again but with no effect as the hero ran up to the duplicates and took them down with swift blows to the head. Back Draft then stepped up from behind the counter and approached the superhero and unleashed the last fart he was able to muster. The hero seemed undeterred and continued, as in his metal form he had no sense of smell.

Back Draft backed off and Mod Doll stepped in, wrapping his limbs around Mr. Molybdenum, not able to slow him in the least. The hero laughed again and pulled off one of Mod Dolls arms, ripping it free of his body. Stuffing floated into the air as the rag doll man let go screaming.

Mr. Molybdenum looked at the villain and said, "You know... I can kill all of you and I'll still be considered a hero? This bank pays us for protection and if I kill the villains who murdered all these guards and whoever the hell these other guys are, the public will think I'm doing a service to everyone. They're not going to release those tapes. So, I guess what I'm saying is... get ready to diiiieee..."

The superhero wasn't paying close enough attention to where he was walking during his maniacle monologue and didn't notice just how close he was walking to the vampire poop on the ground by his feet. It only took a moment as he slipped in the shit while saying the word 'die' and fell flat on his back with enough weight from his metal body to knock the wind out of himself. The thud hit the ground with such a force that it cracked the tiles under him and shook the robotic rabbit suit loose from atop of Death Shriek.

The supervillain didn't waste time or mince words as he got to his feet, ran up to Mr. Molybdenum. and screamed right in his face. The hero looked on in horror as his metallic body cracked and black ooze poured from his ears, eyes and nose. He screamed in turn as his body contorted with the sound of metal folding upon itself. The metal continued to crack until it unexpectedly shattered.

The hero was dead and the day was saved by the serious case of a vampire's assplosion. As the villains recovered, they gathered their money bags and made their way to the invisible car parked out front. Steve noticed Death Shriek handing Mod Doll a hundred dollars as they got into the car.

"What was that about?"

Death Shriek shook his head as everyone piled into the car with the money loaded in the trunk, "Nothing. Don't worry about it. Also sit on your jacket cause I don't want shit all over my upholstery."

So with that, our story draws to a close, providing the conclusive proof to that age old question on whether or not vampires poop. The final answer being:

Yes. Yes they do. Everyone poops except robots.

10.
MYSTERIES FROM A TO Z

In this book we gave the answer to whether or not a vampire poops, but there are still other mysteries in this Universe. Important questions that have gone unanswered for too long and this chapter seeks to remedy this.

Now, it should be said that there are simply too many mysteries in the entire universe to be able to answer all of them in a single volume of a book, so instead we will be answering one mystery per letter of the alphabet. If you are still wondering whether vampires poop, see chapters one through nine for that answer.

However, the mysteries covered here, in alphabetical order, most of them took years of research and experience to come by the answers and at the very least, minutes on the internet to learn the factoids presented to you here today. That being said, I hope you enjoy some of the other mysteries of the universe:

A is for the Aristocrats – There is an old joke called the aristocrats, but what is the point of it and why have I never heard the same version twice?

There is a very good answer to that, but for those who are unfamiliar with the joke it goes as follows:

So a family act goes in to see a talent agent. There was a mother, a father, and two children. They came in and the talent agent asks to see what they do.

The family then proceeds to do the most horrible and unspeakable act ever seen. The mother and father just start punching their kids and then they switch off and the kids start punching and kicking their parents in the head and they keep switching off till everyone is a bloody pulp and only the father remains conscious, even then just barely. The talent agent is shocked and asks what the act is called to which the father says: The Aristocrats.

Now the middle part of the joke where the family performs an unspeakable act can be anything and usually is. The point of the joke is to just make the act as long and horrible as possible, just telling the worst possible thing, with the punchline remaining the same where the name of the act ends up being called: The Aristocrats.

The world record for the longest telling of, and most horrible story ever recorded for the Aristocrats is held by Gilbert Gottfried, who told an uninterrupted sixteen and a half hour version of the joke during the Friars' Club roast of Hugh Hefner in September 2001.

Some who have read this book have told me that they would compare it to the aristocrats in the roundabout way that it arrives at the final answer to whether or not vampires actually poop.

B is for the Brown Note – What is the brown note?

The brown note is a thing of urban legend. It is said that there is a certain sound, that if played to anyone will instantly cause them to poop. It is a sound that was allegedly discovered by Russian scientists near the end of the cold war, with hopes to weaponize it in the field.

However, a countering sound wave was never discovered and research was stopped after the lead scientist shit himself to death in a freak lab accident. The project was abandoned and after the fall of the Soviet Union all research was lost.

Rumor has it that there was a band in the US of A, named Bobby Hornblower and the Uptown Five, in the late 1980s who accidentally played the brown note during a recording session. Everyone present shit their pants every time the song was played back and all recordings of it were confiscated by the CIA. The band was thereafter erased from history, with memories wiped, or so the legend of the brown note goes. Some say that any time there is a one hit wonder, it's because the band discovered the brown note on a later album and were then dismissed by the government and prohibited from attaining any manner of fame from there on out.

C is for Centaur – What exactly makes a centaur and what is the truth behind the legend?

By definition, a centaur is half man half horse, normally with the top half of a man sticking out where the neck of a horse would normally be.

The most famous story from the tales of centaurs told by the ancient Greeks, is that of the Centauromachy. A tale of a family of demigods named the Lapiths who had a wedding where they invited a whole bunch of centaurs...

because, why not? However, unfortunately, the centaurs they had invited were not used to wine and they got real rapey real fast. So the story of the Centauromachy is really the story of a demigod wedding where the bride, groom, and all of the guests had to fight off impending rape from a bunch of horse men. Apparently, the battle became such a favorite theme for artists, as an excuse to display close-packed bodies in violent confrontation, even a young Michelangelo executed a marble bas-relief of the battle in 1492.

Despite the Centauromachy, and all the negative stereotypes of most every centaur story put to a page, there were a few other depictions of them that fell into a positive light. A centaur named Chiron taught Achilles how to play the lyre... and I mean... that's the only one that comes to mind but still there are probably others out there somewhere...

Anywho, mythology aside, some scholars feel that the stories of the centaur originated from non-riding cultures seeing nomads on horseback for the first time.

D is for Doppelganger – I don't understand the joke from the book with the Doppelgangster... what even is a doppelganger?

First of all... nice grammar... but as far as the term doppelganger or, in the original German, doppelgänger goes, it literally means double-goer. It is meant to be interpreted as a look-alike or copy of a living person. They are sometimes portrayed in stories as a paranormal phenomenon and have ordinarily been seen as a harbinger of bad luck. Some traditions insist that the double-goer as an evil twin and some cultures refer to them as a twin stranger.

The word doppelganger is often used in popular culture to describe any person who physically resembles another person. However, the doppelganger is not a modern concept. In ancient Egyptian mythology there were thought to be people called a ka, or spirit double, who had the same memories and feelings of the person they were copied from. In Norse mythology the vardøger is a ghostly double who preceded a living person and performed their actions before they arrived. In China there are also the stories of the Nǐ hěn bèn that were also known as the Wǒ bù fānyì which in English would be called the face rippers and they were terrible beasts from the woods who would rip off the faces of the living so that they could get close to other humans and eat them as they slept.

E is for Exoskeleton - What is an exoskeleton and what is it's purpose?

An exoskeleton is exactly as the name suggests. Exo meaning outside of and skeleton meaning a structure that supports. The exoskeleton is ordinarily a metalic skeletal structure used to support a body when the internal skeletal structure, or endoskeleton, is unable to.

In the case of Black Jack Rabbit, his exoskeleton was mechanically enhanced to give him increased strength and speed and was armored to provide him with enhanced durability. Other examples of superhero characters who utilize special armored exoskeletons are of course the famous Metal Man or Rocket Red.

F is for Frankenstein - Who is this ever famous Frankenstein I keep hearing about?

I'm so glad you asked. I get asked this question a lot actually and the simplest answer to that is... she is my cat. I adopted her as a stray that was born on my grandma's farm and we immediately became the best of friends.

She is a tortie, or tortoise shell colored fur, cat and with that she comes with plenty of what is known in cat circles as: tortitude. With her tortie colorings she actually looked like several cats meshed up into one, so on first meeting her we called her Franken-cat. After Adopting her I decided on the better name of Frankenstein, aka Frankie, named after the very famous cat from Red Dwarf who belonged to Dave Lister in the first episode, and from her children they spawned the entire race of cat people from there on out several million years later.

G is for Goblin - Do Goblins poop?

Yes they do. Also they eat babies usually, if given the opportunity. Alternate spellings for goblin used throughout Europe are gobblin, gobeline, gobling, goblyn and gobbelin... all of which poop.

That feels like a waste of a goblin question though... how about a bonus question that is between the letters G and H in addition to the G and H questions? Absolutely so the question between questions would be - What is the difference between Goblins and Hobgoblins?

Well, there isn't much difference in the two subspecies. Both of them are almost always small, grotesque, mischievous, greedy, and often have magic powers similar to a fairy. The primary difference is that goblins tend to stay outside and hobgoblins tend to hide in people's homes.

The origin of the name hobgoblin actually comes from a single French story of a little house goblin named Crekoll. He was stepped on by an old man, the injury of which hobbled him and they ended up calling him a hobbled goblin during the story and later used the French skill of portmanteau, combining the words into hobgoblin instead. In short, hobgoblins are goblins who live in houses while goblins just live out in the wild instead.

H is for Hell Hound - One hears the term hell hound, but what exactly is a hell hound and where did that term originate?

Odd as it may sound, I did extensive research on hell hounds and their origins for a different book I wrote (called Tales of Impending Peril) and so I have just that information ready for you now.

There are stories of ghost dogs, wolves, and hounds from around the world but the hell hound that we know best, and has come to be the hound used in fantasy literature and television the most, is based on the Welsh legend of the Cwn Annwn (pronounced Key-une Ann-une). They were white and silver furred dogs with brilliantly red ears. They served the god of the underworld, named Arawn, and helped him hunt the souls of the dead to bring back with him to the afterlife in his ghost pouch called the Diafol Sgrotwm. It was Christians who later dubbed the dogs the Hounds of Hell.

In England there were several monsterous and ghostly black dogs that were said to be hell hounds named the Barghest, the Black Shuck, the Gwyllgi, the Black Hound of Destiny, the Yeth Hound, the Gytrash, the Moddey Dhoo or even the Yortlebort. Which ever name was chosen, the dogs were often said to be of giant stature for a hound and that they were often ghostly in appearance. More often than not they were depicted as vicious beasts who would hunt the dead, and the living if they weren't careful to steer clear of them. They were also sometimes thought of as heralds of death or protectors of the dead.

I is for Ipotane - What is an Ipotane?

Well, it is another creature that is a horse/human hybrid, much like the centaurs, but unlike the centaurs they don't seem to be quite so rape happy.

Overall the Ipotane looked like humans but had the legs, hindquarters, tail, ears and teeth of a horse. Although some of the stories describe them with human-like legs instead. If you ask me, and you did, I feel like maybe someone stupid saw a guy with hairy legs, a long fuzzy belt and a hat then said to themselves, "It's a magical creature!" and then the Ipotane came into existence.

J is for Jackalope – How did the Jackalope come to be the cryptozooilogical sensation that it is today?

For those of you who don't know. The jackalope is a creature that looks exactly like an ordinary rabbit but it has the antlers of an antelope so the name itself comes from a combination of the names jack rabbit and antelope.

It is a creature of North American folklore that was invented by a pair of taxidermists named the Herrick brothers in the 1930s who made one as a proof of their taxidermy skills. There was an underlying legend of unknown origins out in the state of Wyoming upon which inspired them to create the creature and it wasn't until they started making and selling jackalopes that the creature gained tremendous popularity and nestled a place in the hearts of the American people.

Since their time the legend of the jackalope has become a many varied and wildly differing story among folklorists world wide. It is also known as the horned rabbit, the ungulate hare, and the pronghorn bunny.

K is for Kraken – What is the Kraken and where did a story like that come from?

The kraken is an old Norwegian story that dates back to the book called the Konungs Skuggsja, written around the year 1250AD, in which the creature is first described and talked about in great detail.

The creature has always been described as a massive cephalopod that was allegedly routinely sighted in the Greenland Sea. People were afraid to mention it's name while at sea lest they summon the kraken. It was described as a massive monster that was so massive that the author thought there must only be two in all of existence for there would be no way for them to get enough food to sustain any more numbers than just the pair of them.

Later sailors said that the body of the kraken had been mistaken for an island on occasion and that the real danger of the beast was from the whirlpools it would leave it its wake. It is normally described as a massive squid or octopus, but sometimes it is said to have a shell on it's back as well. Many television shows, movies, books and other media have since featured the kraken in a variety of shapes, sizes and appearances since.

L is for the Loch Ness Monster – How could the Loch Ness Monster actually go so undetected for all these years and have absolutely no real proof of it existing with all those people searching for it?

An excellent question indeed. First, I feel I should say just what the Loch Ness Monster is and where the legend originated though, for those who are uninformed. Loch Ness sort of a small lake, connected to the ocean, and is located in Scotland. The creature is often depicted as either a massive serpent or as a type of dinosaur known as an Elasmosaur. There has yet to be any solid proof in either photo or video form and everything to date has been disproved as a hoax.

The reason why no thorough search has been conducted from top to bottom extensively… is money. No one has ever dedicated real time or money to the search and until a search with some money behind it is conducted we will likely only have doctored photos to go off of as the only visual proof of Nessie's existence.

M is for Molybdenum – What is Molybdenum?

Molybdenum is the chemical element with the symbol Mo and atomic number 42. It is shiny ordinarily and has a silver colored appearance.

It was once used to make pencils, it is present in dark leafy vegetables and was used to strengthen armor plating during World War I. It is an essential element for life in all higher eukaryote organisms, though there are some bacteria that manage to get by without it. There are only five other elements that have a higher melting point and can be used to reinforce spaceships that have to endure the temperatures of atmospheric reentry.

While there are undoubtedly a number of very smart uses for Molybdenum, interestingly enough, it was actually named by dumb people. It was discovered by the Greek people and it's name is derived from the Ancient Greek Molybdos, which means lead. It was called this because it was so often mistaken for lead when people were digging for metals in the ground. That's right. They named it lead because it was always mistaken for lead. The geniuses who came up with that name became rich and famous, while you on the other hand are stuck here staring at the stupidity of it all with your yammer hole agawk in bewilderment.

N – N is for Novelist - Who wrote this book? Is this book a Novel? What is the difference between a Novel and a Novella... or even a Novelette?

Allow me to answer this one in reverse order. The Difference between a novel or novella comes down to word count. An average mainstream novel nowadays is composed of 60,000 words, with approximately 250 words per page coming to a total of around 240 pages. The bare minimum to be considered novel length would be 40,000 words by the strictest definitions; any book that is between 39.999 words and 17,500 words is considered a novella; any book between 17,499 words and 7,500 words is considered a novelette; if a book is under 7,500 words it is considered a short story. By those classifications, this book is a Novella, while the book entitled: Tales of Impending Peril, is a Novel.

By industry standard, in the past, mass-market fantasy books were between 60,000 to 90,000 words but today the standard sets the books right at 125.000. For new authors, either going to an independent publisher or via literary agent, they often prefer books to be closer to the 80,000 word mark for new authors and ordinarily will never publish a new author if the work of fiction is more than 110,000 words long.

As far as who wrote this particular novella, the novelist, and person who is writing this for you now, is Michael Trupiano. Ordinarily in most any book there is an about the author section and I decided to hide mine within this entry under the letter 'N'.

Michael Trupiano is a man who has written several books for several series of books that, at the time of this publication, still await their audience to find them. He normally sports a mustache and goatee. Additionally, he has the ability to grant anyone the power of flight but has yet to find anyone he deemed worthy of the gift.

He is also of the belief that no one ever reads the about the author sections of books all the way through and has been known to write in nonsense while placing his own within the books he has written.

O is for Ouroboros – What is the Ouroboros meant to represent?

The Ouroboros is a world famous snake, serpent, or dragon who is depicted eating its own tail, forever growing and just eating itself in an eternal circle. It is a symbol meant to represent the infinite cycle of nature's endless creation and destruction. A symbol of life and death. One would have to hope that the ouroboros does not need to poop or that would be very gross and awkward though.

P is for Poltergeist – I've heard the term before, but what is the difference between a Poltergeist and your every day run of the mill ghost?

A ghost is an other-worldly entity that is a person who was formerly alive but they stuck around after they died; sometimes because of unfinished business, sometimes because of a curse, and sometimes because they just felt like it. A poltergeist is a ghost who is normally very angry and violent. The tend to make a lot of noise and displace physical object more than the regular haunting sort of ghost.

Many people will tell you that poltergeist literally translates to noisy ghost, but what it actually translates to is chicken ghost. If you have ever been around a chicken before, you know they can be annoyingly loud. That is why it was the creature chosen to describe this particular very noisy type of ghost.

Q is for Qilin – What are those dog/dragon statues that I see at Chinese restaurants, monuments, and buildings?

Those would be a representation of the Qilin. A mystical beast who is a mixture of dragon and deer, also called a kirin. A sort of chimera that is said to appear before the arrival of a great person or ruler. Often depicted with antlers, like many Chinese dragons, and is most often depicted as either gold in color or every color of the rainbow.

They are divine animals and much like a unicorn, they will only allow a virgin to approach them. There is of course the famous story of the mischievous child Wang Fang who delighted in sneaking laxative herbs into the tea of the village elders. He did this so much that their tears summoned a Qilin to correct the child. The child was then followed for a number of years by the mystical beast and every time he acted up in poked him in the butt with it's antlers. One day, with his hindquarters rendered raw by the Qilin, he stopped his mischievous ways and vowed to respect his elders, sparing him further pain and misfortune.

The Qilin then granted him a ride on it's back and they flew over the countryside as a present to the boy for changing his wicked ways.

R is for Reading - What exactly is reading?

Reading is the ability a human mind, and possibly some other minds in the animal and alien kingdoms, posses to translate pictorial images into words that are understood. Some people cannot read but if you are reading this then surely you must know what reading is. Right?

What did you think you were doing? Eating a cake? How is that even possible? Reading and cake are two separate things. I mean... sometimes you can read something on a cake, if someone wrote something on it. However, you cannot cake something on a read, to my knowledge.

Also, I searched a whole bunch more... I couldn't find any other centaur stories where things didn't get rapey. I guess that is just what their stories were about. Creepy right?

S is for Smoking – What is the proper way to partake in tobacco?

There isn't merely one way to partake, but rather several ways, each requiring different levels of skill, all of which are packed with carcinogens and give the risk of catching a pesky case of the cancers though.

As a former tobacco connoisseur I leaned many a thing or two over the years about cigarettes, cigars, pipes, hookahs, and a variety of tobacco based products. All of which are bad for you but some of which can be a pleasant treat if used in moderation.

Cigarettes, or fags as the British call them, are more for the avid addict. Someone who is addicted to coffin nails utilizes them mostly for stress relief, appetite suppression, pleasure, and to feed the chemical addiction that forms from partaking in a lot of Nicotine. Nicotine itself has been proven to be one of the most addictive substances on the planet. The only things more addictive are barbiturates, cocaine, alcohol, heroin, cortexiphan and byphodine.

Cigars are more of a celebratory tobacco product; regularly partaken by expecting fathers, business tycoons, pretentious know-it-alls, general bad-asses and Hellboys alike. They are not meant to be inhaled deeply like a cigarette would be, but rather to be slowly puffed on and enjoyed. Slowly puffed upon over longer periods of time, the cigar can actually be extinguished and reignited for a new flavor that some prefer, while if you tried the same with a cigarette, you might as well try to burn some wet dog hair wrapped up in newspaper.

Hookahs and pipes are devices for the more advanced tobacconist simply because of all the work that goes into the proper usage of them. A hookah, also known as a hubbly-bubbly in some of the more elite hookah circles, is a device where you set a gel-moistened tobacco atop a burner, cover it in foil, and then set a burning coal atop it.

There are hoses submerged under water, in the main body of the device, that tobacconist sucks the tobacco smoke through. It is not advised to use a hookah on your own and if it is your first time trying one, I highly recommend a hookah bar instead.

Pipes are a monster all their own. Truly the most difficult of the tobacco appliances to master. One wrong move and you will simply not enjoy the fragrant experience you so want from the intoxicating scent of that pipe tobacco The pipe itself is the first thing that you want to get right. You want to ensure that there is good airflow from the bottom of the pipe itself by placing a mesh metal screen on the bottom.

The next thing is how you pack the tobacco into the pipe. Pipe tobacco comes in a bag as a sort of loose leaf tobacco To properly put it into the pipe you would pack it in three times. The first time, you fill it to the top and push in lightly; the second time you fill it to the top and push down medium hard; and the third time you fill to the top you press down hard. After doing so you would want to either use a toothpick, or a special pipe tool called a wilbideedoo to adjust the tobacco to ensure good airflow to the holes under the metal mesh. Then there you go... after a properly packed pipe is set then you are off to the races like Jeeves and Wooster.

I actually learned everything I know about pipes and pipe tobacco from a man named Jim who dressed exceedingly fancy. He told me an easy system to remember how to pack the tobacco into a pipe. He said: Pack it like a baby, pack it like a boy, then pack it like a man. He showed me a number of tricks to manipulate the tobacco in the pipe with his wilbideedoo with great skill and proficiency, the likes of which I have seen before or since. Fancy Jim was a wise man indeed.

T is for Turpentine – Where did Turpentine come from?

Well, the word for turpentine comes from the Latin turp meaning removal, en meaning of, and tine meaning paint. There are a variety of types of turpentine, all of which are referred to as the turps by people in the chemistry fields. As for the substance itself, it is a wood based compound that was discovered by accident in the late nineteenth century during a massive forest fire.

By boiling the sap of certain industry secret trees in copper pots, they are able to distill the paint stripping substance. It was also originally sold by snake oil salesmen as one of the components of a cure-all they developed called Timey Joe's Body Cleanser. Due to the excess amount of deaths tied to the product it was quickly removed from the market by mobs of angry people who burned the chemical factory to the ground in 1897.

U is for Ultraviolet – What is ultraviolet radiation and why should I be worried about it?

Not to be confused with a movie by the same name, Ultraviolet the Radiation is actually a type of electromagnetic radiation with a wavelength between that of visible light and x-rays. It actually makes up about ten percent of the total light output by the sun. It is also output by black lights, tanning lamps, mercury vapor lamps, and certain electric arcs. We do need UV radiation for our bodies to produce the bone-strengthening vitamin D but, like many things, in excess it can be dangerous.

It can cause sun burns, skin cancer, and dangerous mutations that may possibly result in super powers, but more often than not actually turn people into giant piles of mush called Uvaniks. It has also been determined that UV rays are the cause behind spontaneous human combustion.

V is for Vampire – What do you mean, vampires poop? How can that be?

It's true. They do. If you don't believe me then see chapters one through nine. Proof that they do, but for those who care to delve even further, I'll provide a brief explanation on that as well.

Just like you and every other human, or whichever earthbound form of higher intelligence, they possess a digestive tract. They have a mouth, an esophagus, a stomach, intestines, and even a tranglemork.

They take their food, in the form of blood, into their mouth, swallow and digest it for sustenance. Then after that blood nourishes the vampire's undead body through an ancient magic process called eupepsia; from the Latin eu, meaning 'to steal', pep, meaning 'the power from', and sia, meaning 'with magic'.

You can always tell the difference between a vampire's poop and a human's poop by the fact that the smell has a distinctly rusty scent to it. The appearance has been likened to that of a human's own fecal matter after eating an entire red velvet cake. Another little known fact is that the street slang for vampire poop is: crapula.

W is for Werewolf – Are werewolves just mindless beasts or do they maintain a part of their former self after the transformation to half person and half wolf?

Depending on the story being told, some breeds of werewolves (also called wolfmen, lycanthropes, lycans, yortlemorks or krublems) change during times of the full moon alone, or they can change at will.

I have found that in stories where the wolf change is a curse then the werewolf becomes a mindless killing machine. However, when a wolf changes at will, then the are able to retain themselves and their mind while in wolf form.

In stories where they can change at will but are forced to change during the full moon against their will, then the willful change retains their mind but the forced change reverts them to the mindless killing machine type of werewolf.

A common misconception about werewolves is that they prey solely on humans, when in fact their favorite food is actually beef. Speaking of beef that brings up another question that is worth mentioning: Where did the phrase: 'Where's the beef?' come from?

The answer is not well advertised nor known by many at all. In the early 1980s there was a billionaire in Texas named Benson Whorley who had a vision. He was oil rich and at 97 years of age, many thought he suffered from dementia. He spent millions of dollars of his company's money to make an amusement park to combat the rise of vegetarianism.

He called it Meat Land and it was an amusement park made almost entirely out of beef and beef byproducts against the advice of everyone who was consulted. Within a week it was declared an environmental disaster area. Within two weeks it was lost to the vultures who were thick enough to black out the sun.

Meat Land is now in the area of Texas called Vulture Island. It's a lost skeleton city where divorced ghost dads take their kids on the weekend and ask inappropriate questions about their ex's new boyfriend.

The massive beef shortage that was caused by building a small town almost entirely from beef created a serious beef shortage and a popular catchphrase all at once. 'Where's the beef?' has since been used as a slogan for promotion by the North American beef cow farmers.

X is for Xamantha – Wait a minute... who or what is Xamantha?

Xamantha is a pudding pack stealing fool. I know you have been eating my pudding out of the office fridge Xamantha. That's right. I saw you. It had my name on it and you ate them all relentlessly. That was my pudding.

Y is for Yeti – What is the difference between a Yeti and a Sasquatch?

The truth of the matter is that both of them are different types of the same creature, as is big foot. It's just a regional name. Different areas of the globe call them different things but in reality the Yeti, or abominable snowman, and the Sasquatch, or big foot, are the same kind of creature.

Z is for Zorbulak the Destroyer, Dark Lord of the Seven Mountains of Kothuur and Horde Master of the Jeethos'akun – Is that the same dragon, named Zorbulak the Ever Fluffy, that I remember from my childhood?

Why as a matter of fact it is the same Zorbulak. A lot happened to Zorbulak after his television series was canceled. He went down some dark roads and couldn't turn back again...

The End.

AN AFTERWARDS BY FRANKENSTEIN THE CAT

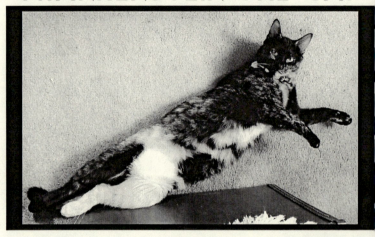

lllllllllllllllppppppppppppppppppppppppppppppppppppppp
ppppppppppppppppppppppppppppppppkkkkkkkkkkkkkkkkk
kkkkkkkkkkkkkkkkkkkkkkkkkkkkkkkkkkkkkkkkkkkkkkkkk
kkkkkkkkkkkkkkkkkkkkkkkkkkkkkkkkkkkkkkkkkkkkkkkkk
kkkkkkkkkkkkkkkkkkkkkkkkkkkkkkkkkjjjjjjjjjjjhgflllllllllll
llllllllllllllllllllllllllllllllllllllllllllllllllllllllllllllllllllllllllllll
lllllllllllllllllllllllllllllllllllllllllllllllllllllllllllllllllllllll88
88888888888888888888888888888888888888888888888
88888888888888888888888888888888888888888888888
88888888888888888888888888888888888888888888888
88888888888888888888888888888888888888888888888
888888888888888888888888888lllllllllllllllllllllllllllllll
lllllllccccccccccccccccccccccccccccccccccccccccccccccc
ccccccccccccccccccccccccccccccccccccccccccccccccccc
ccccccccccssssssssssssssssssssssssssssssssssssssssssss
ssssssssssssssssssssssssssssssssssssssssssssssssssssss
sssssssssssssss   gh

Other Radio Galaxy Classics:

* Tales of Impending Peril
    Vol 1. The Fires of Hexmalivus

* Alistair and the All-Purpose Umbrella
    Vol 1.
    Vol 2.
    Vol 3.
    Vol 4.

* The Adventures of Race Wilcox

* Heavy Metal Massacre

* Edwin the Dogtective
    The Submarine Contingency
    Mystery on the Indian Pacific
    The Flying Pigs of Regina

* Six Minutes to Midnight

* Single Dollar Purchase

__Coming Soon From Radio Galaxy Publications__

* Tales of Impending Peril
    * Vol 2. Heralds of the Vicious Dark
    * Vol 3. Legion of Moonfire
    * Vol 4. Epoch of the Seventh Mind

* Firenado

* Periwinkle Plumb

* Dime's Dozen Deadly Dames

* The Space Lighthouse

Until next time...

CPSIA information can be obtained
at www.ICGtesting.com
Printed in the USA
FSOW01n1228251117
41642FS